see notes p. "ö"

A Small Masterpiece

A Small Masterpiece

TIM HEALD

PUBLISHED FOR THE CRIME CLUB BY
DOUBLEDAY & COMPANY, INC.
GARDEN CITY, NEW YORK
1982

All of the characters in this book
are fictitious, and any resemblance
to actual persons, living or dead,
is purely coincidental.

ACKNOWLEDGMENTS

The lines from T. S. Eliot are from *Whispers of Immortality* in COLLECTED POEMS 1909–1962 by T. S. Eliot; copyright, 1936, by Harcourt Brace Jovanovich, Inc., copyright © 1963, 1964 by T. S. Eliot. Reprinted by permission of the publishers, Harcourt Brace Jovanovich, Inc. and Faber & Faber Ltd.

The lines from John Betjeman are from *The Varsity Students' Rag* and *I.M. Walter Ramsden O.B., March 26, 1947, Pembroke College Oxford* in COLLECTED POEMS by John Betjeman. Reprinted by permission of the publishers, John Murray, Ltd.

Library of Congress Cataloging in Publication Data

Heald, Tim.
A small masterpiece.

I. Title.
PR6058.E167S6   823'.914
AACR2
ISBN 0-385-17942-1
Library of Congress Catalog Card Number 81–43394

First Edition in the United States of America

A Small Masterpiece

for the Master of
. BALLIOL
from Tim Groad

Nov. 2, 1991

P.54 anonymous 'Balliol' gents. wearing Balliol scarves.

P.61 Bognor mistaken for Balliol man

P.63. reference to A.B - likes secretly

P.76 Willis Bund, Dean of Balliol
      is cited

P.90 Back gate of Balliol

p.9. Names on staircases written as they are
      at Balliol

In ~ 1993 I wrote to Tim Heald and asked him
if he had meant that the women on p.54 were
in fact Balliol persons. He said they were
          BGB.

It was first light in the garden quad of Apocrypha. Because this was an English summer no rosy fingers gave earnest of the dawn, which arrived instead grey and misty and by stealth, creeping up on night like a mugger after an old lady's handbag. Water dripped from the mulberries and splashed plangently from a broken drainpipe over the west door of Hawksmoor's incomparable college chapel. At the foot of the steps leading up to Great Hall a puddle had formed. Through it walked the Master. He was oblivious to the wet for he was drunk, so drunk that he scarcely noticed the dampness which seeped through the splits in his patent leather shoes and ran in tiny rivulets down his neck and under the stiff white collar of his boiled white shirt.

He staggered slightly as he walked across his quad: Lord Beckenham of Penge, master of all he surveyed, a self-made man made good. He had come a long way from the council estate in Skelmersdale. If, at seventy-one, that mane of white hair, so envied by his older colleagues, was finally thinning, and if those once so regular teeth were now a little chipped and yellow, he could still claim them as his own. Own teeth, own hair, own everything. He was his own man. Always had been.

Thus he reflected as he slowly crossed the quad, and so immersed was he in these thoughts (and so fuddled with claret and liqueurs) that he did not notice another figure, similarly clad, similarly uncertain in its gait, emerge from the shadows at the bottom of staircase twelve. Half-way across the quad the two almost collided.

"Ah, Aveline," exclaimed Lord Beckenham, recovering first and recognising the gaunt features of the Regius Professor of Sociology. "Agreeable Gaudy."

"Very," said Aveline. "I've been up drinking with Badman and Scrimgeour-Harris."

"And I with Mitten's men," said the Master. "Edgware, Vole, Rook, Crutwell and Bognor."

"Ah . . . Bognor," murmured Aveline dreamily. "But otherwise a good year."

"A very good year," agreed Lord Beckenham, then paused. "Can I offer you a nightcap?"

"That's very kind but no. I've a bicycle to catch." The professor laughed harshly, like a corncrake, the noise echoing over the grass. He moved on. "Cheerio, then," he called unexpectedly.

The Master continued on his way, though without enthusiasm. The Lodgings had been gloomy since Mabel's death three years ago, and despite the hour he was not particularly keen to get to bed. There were three flights of stairs to negotiate, too, and they were steep. Recently he had found that they left him distressed and breathless and he was obliged to pause from time to time to gather strength. Time was when he would have taken them three at a time. More than fifty years ago he had come to Apocrypha as a soft-faced freshman on an open scholarship, the first boy from his school ever to win a place at Oxford. The three photographs were still on the wall of the drawing room. In the last of them he sat in the middle of the team, holding the ball, hair parted in the middle, slicked down like Hitler's. He had scored the winning goal the last time Apocrypha won cuppers. He unlocked the front door at the third attempt and began to climb. One more Gaudy to go, he thought to himself . . . a farewell Gaudy with his own contemporaries, those few that survived . . . he fumbled with his tie . . . it was too tight . . . it was empty vanity to persist with the old collar he had worn so long . . . far too tight . . . he stopped to rest and swayed slightly, then clung to the rail for support . . .

The scout found him when he came with morning tea.

He was, of course, extremely dead.

CHAPTER 1

Bognor was awoken by bells. He had forgotten what a bell-ridden city Oxford was. He had similar trouble with Venice. "Bloody bell," he muttered and, raising his head slightly, he removed the pillow and buried his head underneath it. The bells were now muffled but they were still disturbing. Bognor cursed them again and put out an arm, seeking the consolation of his wife, Monica. She was not there. He sighed, sat up, letting the pillow fall to the floor, and, very tentatively, opened an eye, shutting it again immediately. He was not ready to have light thrown upon his situation, which was, he was beginning to realise, hung-over in the extreme. The furry sensation in his mouth and throat told him that he had been over-indulging in drink and tobacco. This was confirmed by the ache behind the eyes. He scratched his scalp and attempted to coax the memory into some form of action. It stalled a couple of times but at the third try he was able to recall a little of the night before. Of course. The Gaudy. He had adjourned with his old colleagues from Mitten's tutorial group. The port had run out. They had gone to Mitten's rooms in the Pantry Quad. The Master had been there too. And that extraordinarily attractive new English don. Hermione something. Clacton? Southend? Margate? No, none of that was right but it was a place somewhere down there. Frinton, that was it. He remembered Mitten introducing them. "Bognor and Frinton," he said in that affected aristocratic drawl of his, "Well, you two ought to have lots in common, eh? Ha! Ha!" He was the only person Bognor had ever met who, when intending to convey the idea of laughter, actually said, "Ha! Ha!"—two separate words, clearly articulated, rather as if he had been taught to laugh by some do-it-yourself manual for foreign students.

"Oh dear, oh dear, oh dear!" With a supreme effort Bognor forced both eyes open and let them slowly traverse the room. It was a newish bed-sitter, on the site of what had once been a damp, draughty, Victorian tower full of Bognor's memories. There was the obligatory poster of Che in his beret and of Monroe with fluorescent lips and, he was depressed to see, even of "girl in tennis dress scratching bottom." An Apocrypha undergraduate ought to be able to manage a little more originality than that. It was a bit like having flying ducks or that green woman painted by the Russian whose name he could never remember. The one you saw in Woolies. He looked at his watch 9:15 A.M. Better put in an appearance at breakfast. That insufferable Crutwell would have been out for his ghastly jog by now. Edgware too, in all probability. They'd both be looking pink and scrubbed and young for their age and generally disgusting. The trouble with this reunion was that it was making him feel a failure. He *was* a failure. He knew that; but this reminded him of the fact all too forcibly. Not only was he a failure, he looked like one alongside all these budding success stories.

He swung his legs out, touched the floor with his toes and tried standing. Not a good idea. He sat down again and passed a palm over his jowls. All his problems stemmed from university. It was that absurd interview with the Appointments Board which had got him into the Board of Trade in the first place, since when he had been stuck. Codes, ciphers, red tape and occasional excursions into what was euphemistically described as "the field."

He had had his moments, he supposed. Parkinson had even mentioned the possibility of an MBE recently, though he had resisted all Bognor's requests for a transfer to some other branch of Whitehall. Monica was urging him with increasing fervour to "get out while there's still time" but nothing happened. He made a few half-hearted enquiries and even went to one (very depressing) job interview at some multi-national. It came, of course, to nothing. Secretly Bognor knew that he had left it too late and that he was doomed to the Board of Trade for life. He could eventually take early retirement and live on his index-linked pension. A depressing future stretched ahead, a depressing past lay behind, and a depressing present enveloped him. It was all made much worse by the Apocrypha Gaudy and renewed acquaintance with his contemporaries.

Outside, the bells ceased. He stood again and staggered over to the washbasin where he recoiled sharply from the reflection which leered back at him from the mirror. Thank the Lord, it wasn't a full-length one. He scratched his stomach and realised that it was sagging flabbily over the cord of his pyjamas. They were the same pyjamas he had had when he was at Oxford twenty years ago. They didn't make them like that any more, stout striped flannel pyjamas designed to last a lifetime. The manufacturers had not, however, bargained on Bognor's increasing girth. It was rather sad to find oneself growing out of one's pyjamas. He frowned into the mirror and told himself brusquely not to be so wet. Life was just beginning. Couple of aspirin, a shave and brisk clean of the teeth and he'd be a new man. He remembered Crutwell and Edgware and their fitness mania. For a second he even contemplated the idea of a press-up, but the thought passed quickly. Too late to start that sort of thing now.

When he reached Hall he found that, as he had feared, his friends were already heavily involved with a hearty breakfast. Even Sebastian Vole, Associate Professor of Modern History at Prendergast in Vermont, was chomping cornflakes, and he was reputed to only come alive at noon. There was a chorus of "Mornings," "Hello,

Simons," and "Sleep well, old boys?". Bognor replied with an all-embracing grin and poured himself a cup of coffee. A scout offered him cereal and he declined.

"Bacon and egg, sir?"

Bognor suppressed a keen desire to retch.

"Thanks, no," he said, "I'm not really much of a one for breakfast."

"You never showed up for your run," called Ian Edgware. "It was fabulous out on Port Meadow. All river mist and lemon-coloured sun." Edgware had always had a penchant for second-rate imagery. Bognor recalled his verses in some long-defunct literary magazine of their generation. Excruciating.

"Run?" he asked. "What run?"

"You said you were coming for a run, you lazy sod," said Peter Crutwell through a mouthful of toast and marmalade. "Quite definite about it, you were. Said you never missed your morning mile."

"I never." Bognor flushed.

"You did, you know," insisted Crutwell. He was a schoolmaster these days. Highly successful. A "housebeak," as he insisted on calling himself, at Ampleside but not expected to stay much longer. He had been short-listed for the headmastership of Sherborne and Cranlingham and was said to be a virtual certainty for Fraffleigh. Five years there and he would walk into the top job at Eton, Harrow or Winchester and from there to an Oxbridge Mastership, Director-Generalship of the IBA or some other glamorous high-profile public office. Bognor could see it all.

"I'm afraid you did, actually," agreed Vole, glancing up from his cornflakes. "Port talking, but you did say you'd go running with them."

"Oh." Bognor frowned. He had not the slightest recollection of saying any such thing. He turned to Humphrey Rook for confirmation. Humphrey was at least losing his hair, which was some consolation. What remained was black and greasy and brushed straight back off the fore-head. He also had a bit of a paunch, though his expensive banker's suiting made a passable attempt of disguising it.

"My recollection," said Rook, "is that you were in two minds about whether to go running with Ian and Peter or come to Holy Communion with me. You were certainly going to do one or the other, conceivably both, but in the event it seems you did neither. You had a lie-in instead." Rook, who had been a student Trot before such things became fashionable, was now a born-again C of E communicant and a Conservative Parliamentary candidate.

"Nothing wrong with that," said Vole, finishing off his bacon, "I had a bit of a lie-in myself."

"Only a bit of one," said Edgware. "Besides, I hear you were up till five, playing poker with Badman and Scrimgeour-Harris."

"Five-fifteen, actually," said Vole, smiling smugly.

"Well, there you are then," said Edgware with an air of triumph.

"Where?" asked Crutwell.

Bognor poured himself another cup of coffee and wished to God they would all shut up. He had forgotten the incessant chatter which went with Oxford. Yak, yak, yak. How they adored the sound of their own voices! How he hated it! How his head hurt! How sick he felt! How much worse the coffee was making him! He wished Monica had packed Alka-Seltzer as well as aspirin.

"Do you mind if I join you?"

It was the Frinton woman. Bognor was in no condition to leap to his feet, besides which, leaping to one's feet while sitting at an Apocrypha bench with your legs under an Apocrypha table is never easy. Instead, he, like his friends, make a half-hearted gesture, a sort of half knee bend, which Miss Frinton (*Ms.* Frinton? wondered Bognor, *Mrs.* Frinton?) waved away with genial contempt.

"Bad news, I'm afraid," she said, sliding her legs across

the bench and under the table. They were very long and slim, encased in tight, tailored jeans and thigh-length boots.

"Bad news?" said Vole blearily. "Bad? Very bad? Or catastrophic?"

"It's the Master," said Miss Frinton (who was actually entitled to be called *Dr.* Frinton but countenanced no such thing from anyone except her bank manager and the occasional Leavisite). "He's dead."

There was a dramatic silence. For a second no one even swallowed.

"Did you say dead?" asked Bognor, at the end of this eloquently unspoken tribute to the late Lord Beckenham.

"Yes," she said, "dead." She poured herself coffee. "Scout found him when he went in with his morning tea. Sounds like heart. He'd had trouble with his ticker."

"Had he . . . I mean, when, exactly . . . ?" This from Crutwell.

"Never even got to bed," said Hermione breezily. She had a strong-boned, equine quality which suggested she was not easily fazed, even by death. "Struggled up the stairs, four sheets to the wind and keeled over on the landing."

"Not a bad way to go," said Rook, smiling weakly. "Funny, though, I thought he was on pretty good form last night."

"What happens when a Master dies in office?" asked Edgware.

"What do you mean—*happens?*" Hermione Frinton put her head back slightly in order, so it seemed, to squint down her exaggeratedly long (though elegant) nose with an expression of some contempt.

Edgware shrugged. "I mean, who takes over?"

"There'll be some sort of caretaker," said Vole, who had gone rather white, "until there's an election. It happened at Prendergast."

"That's hardly a reliable precedent," said Rook.

"Presumably the senior fellow caretakes," said Bognor, "or takes care."

"No," said Hermione Frinton, "not since they started the Vice-Master scheme. Nowadays he automatically takes over in a situation like this."

"So who's *Vice*-Master?" Edgware seemed undiplomatically irritated.

"Waldegrave," said Hermione. "The job rotates. He's been Vice-Master for a week."

"The Honourable Waldegrave Mitten. Master of Apocrypha," said Rook. "He'll like that."

"Poor old Beckenham," murmured Bognor, but no one paid any attention.

He disliked Mondays as much as the next man, and after a weekend out of town they always came as a more than usually bloody surprise. He had driven back to London after breakfast, arriving just before noon at the flat where he found Monica in bed with the Sunday papers. He was at first displeased by this, but after a brief and, he felt, necessary, show of pique he threw aside the Sunday papers and took their place. An hour or so later the newspapers were retrieved, and, what with one thing and another, they never did get properly dressed, only leaving bed for long enough to cook and eat a couple of steaks and drink a bottle of Banda Azul. They then retreated to the bedroom with two glasses, a bottle of Rémy Martin, and the television, for which Monica had recently bought remote control. In the end it was as pleasant a day as Bognor could remember. It quite restored his faith in life. This had waned considerably at the Apocrypha Gaudy and even his quite genuine affection, indeed, on occasion, lust and, yes, love for his accommodating spouse and had been temporarily eclipsed by Dr. Frinton, the new English don. (He had become aware of her doctorate when passing the bottom of her staircase and seeing her name writ large in white paint on black.) Dr. Frinton did have everlasting

↑ Names on staircase written in this manner at B

legs and also a certain supercilious *hauteur* which, frankly, he fancied. He enjoyed dominating females, but now that he was home again, he had to confess that he was pleased to be back in the bosom of his wife where he belonged. She was a thoroughly good sort, Monica. Not just a pretty face. Not *even* a pretty face, come to that, though perhaps that was being unduly ungallant. She had her failings, God knew, but they had been together so long now that these were almost attractive.

Monday morning, therefore, came as a more than usually unpleasant douche. It began before breakfast with a telephone call.

"Only one man in the world makes a telephone ring like that." Bognor winced. "Can you answer it, darling?"

Monica entered the bedroom brushing her teeth.

"Why should I?" she protested, foaming at the mouth, "I don't want to talk to him, and he doesn't want to talk to me."

"Please." Bognor pressed fingers to his temple. The Rioja and the Rémy, to say nothing of his wife, had been wonderful at the time but it meant a hangover two days running. "Tell him I'm in conference," he hissed.

"Don't be ridiculous. He'll know you're here and refusing to talk to him." Monica spat into her toothmug. "All right. I'll tell him you're here and you refuse to talk to him."

"Right," Bognor said viciously, "you say just that. I'm fed up with him pestering me at all hours of the day and night." He turned over and pulled the blankets over his head. Then, as Monica picked up the receiver and the ringing ceased, he hurriedly emerged again and grabbed the machine from her before she could utter.

"Yes," he answered thickly.

"Bognor?" Bognor grimaced. He was right as usual. The Scotch terrier yap of his immediate superior was what he had expected, and it was what he was now hearing. It whined aggressively at him from the earpiece, causing him to start and hold the machine away from his head for a few moments until he judged it safe to bring it back to closer proximity.

"There's no need to shout," he said. "Yes. Bognor here. At your disposal. What can I do for you?"

"Truly, Bognor, you are a remarkable phenomenon. Death dogs your footsteps, wouldn't you say, in a manner of speaking?"

Bognor glanced up at his wife and made circling gestures with his unoccupied index finger, then followed these with further gestures intended to convey the notion of drinking. He was badly in need of some coffee. Monica made one of her "Oh, for heaven's sake, get it yourself" faces, but retired in the direction of the kitchen, presumably to grind beans.

"I'm sorry," Bognor said into the telephone, "I'm not sure I've got your drift."

"Am I not correct in thinking that you attended the Gaudy of your old college on Saturday night?"

"Yes."

"And, further, that the college in question is Apocrypha, Oxford?"

"Yes."

"And that the Master of Apocrypha is . . . was . . . Lord Beckenham of Penge?"

"Oh. I see. Yes. Lord Beckenham passed away after dinner. But he was seventy-one. And he'd had a dicky ticker. A heart condition. He could have gone any time. My presence was entirely coincidental."

"I wish I could agree, Bognor."

Bognor frowned. In the middle distance there was the sound of beans being ground. "What are you driving at?" he asked.

"You tell me Lord Beckenham died from a heart attack?"

"That's what I was told."

"Well, I have news for you, Bognor. My information is

that the post-mortem shows otherwise. Your old Master was murdered."

"Oh, really." Bognor was quite peeved. "Someone's been having you on. They haven't had time for a post-mortem yet."

"Arranged through the good offices of the Fellow in Clinical Pathology."

"I see." Bognor was inclined to say this when stalling for time. He did not see, and Parkinson knew that he did not see. It was a convention.

"I'm delighted to hear it," said his boss, "because it's more than I do. I'd be grateful if you would step around at your earliest convenience. I'm afraid someone calling himself Doctor the Honourable Waldegrave Mitten is calling on us ere long."

"I don't understand." Bognor was prepared for once to concede defeat. "Why is Mitten coming to see you? Lord Beckenham has nothing to do with the Board of Trade. It's a police matter. Nothing to do with us."

Monica reappeared with coffee, which she handed to him, at the same time pressing a finger to his lips. He was beginning to sound tetchy. It was not good for him, not for Parkinson. One of her roles in life as Mrs. Bognor was to keep him calm.

"As a matter of actual historical fact, Bognor, Lord Beckenham was once, very briefly, Secretary of State for this department. I'm bound to say it was not a happy experience for the department. Nor, I suppose, for Lord Beckenham. But that's by the way. What I have to tell you, Bognor, is that the demise of Lord Beckenham of Penge, God rest his soul, does have something to do with the Board of Trade, and that something is you. Do I make myself clear? So enough of this shilly-shallying, and get round here PDQ."

The phone went dead. Bognor stared at it for a moment, vengefully, then returned it to its cradle and took a slug of coffee. His wife was now sitting on the end of the bed painting her nails.

"You never used to paint your nails before you married me," he said.

"I have to employ all my feminine wiles to make sure you don't stray." She smiled up at him. "Do you want to go back to bed?"

"Yes, but it's out of the question. That was Parkinson. He says the Master didn't just die, he was killed."

"Gosh."

"You don't sound very surprised."

"With you I'm never surprised. You ought to know that by now. I'd be much more surprised if you were able to go to an Oxford reunion and come back *without* leaving at least one corpse behind. I'm surprised you showed such moderation."

"You sound just like Parkinson. Besides, it's not funny. Poor old chap's dead, after all."

"Yes. Who do you think did it?"

"Haven't the foggiest."

Monica put down her paintbox and brush. "Darling," she said, "you're going to have to have the foggiest before too long, because it seems to me that the murderer is almost certain to be someone you know—or knew—moderately well. A contemporary, in fact."

"And they're going to ask me to help them find out who? Set a thief to catch a thief."

"Something like that."

This, therefore, represented a particularly bad start to a traditionally bad day. Worse, if anything, was to come.

Thanks partly to Parkinson's telephone call and subsequent discussion with Monica, Bognor was late and had to take a taxi. This cost over three pounds, putting him in an even viler mood than the one with which he had started. Pounding through the subterranean corridors of the Board of Trade, he collided with the tea lady, upsetting hot water over himself. Arriving at his office, wiping at his trousers with a filthy handkerchief, swearing the while, he was astonished to find a smarmy individual in a pinstripe suit sitting at his desk. The interloper gazed up at him with an air of profoundly irritating self-confidence.

"Yes?" he said, cocking an eyebrow at him.

"What do you mean, 'Yes'?" Bognor did not normally shout, but this was an exception. "This is my office. This is my desk. That is my umbrella stand and that is my personal copy of *Who's Who*, paid for with my own personal money. And that's my tin of Earl Grey. Not to mention, *my* Bitschwiller Champagne poster and *my* Crufts' poster. They are souvenirs."

"Sorry," said the intruder languidly, "Must be some mistake. I was told you were in Oxford on a case. That is, if you're Bognor. Parkinson said you were likely to be in Oxford all week."

"Did he indeed?" Bognor wondered whether to seize the man by the lapels and remove him by force. He decided against it. Not that he doubted his ability to do so, but he did not want to make a scene. Parkinson would not like it. "And who the hell *are* you anyway?"

"My name's Lingard."

"Lingard who?"

"Lingard nobody. I'm Basil Lingard. How do you do?"

"Not at all well. What's your position? What are you doing here? Where are you from?"

"Same as you. More or less. Special Investigator. I'm from Teddington Branch."

"Teddington Branch?" Bognor swallowed. Teddington, variously known as the Lilac Lubianka or Stalag Luft Thames, was a sort of SS to the Board of Trade's Wehrmacht. They were crack troops, hard men, marked "for emergency use only."

"Yes," said Lingard, "Teddington." He smiled, evidently under the impression that his provenance gave him the advantage.

"There's obviously some mistake." Bognor wished he could inject a little more certainty into his voice. "I shall have to discuss it with Parkinson."

"You do that." Lingard grinned and brushed dust from his lapel in a gesture which was clearly intended to be symbolic.

Bognor did not smile back. "I most certainly will," he snapped, and swung on his heel.

For once he did not knock on the door of Parkinson's office, but barged straight past his startled secretary and into the sanctum, almost in one movement. He was very angry indeed. Once in Parkinson's office, however, his nerve failed somewhat. Parkinson did not even look up, and although Bognor recognised this as a hackneyed old Parkinson opening gambit he was still disconcerted by it.

"Do sit down, Bognor," said Parkinson, continuing to write on a lined pad of foolscap.

Bognor fixed the portrait of the Queen with an insolent stare. It was curiously foreign of Parkinson to keep a portrait of Her Majesty above his desk. Not something that was generally done in Whitehall.

"We leave that kind of chauvinism to the Bulgarians," Ian Edgware had told him at the weekend. "Understatement is all." Not for nothing was Edgware talked of as a coming man at the FO. He made the men of Munich look like ravaging Huns or those unpronounceable European émigrés who were always popping up in the White House to bolster lame-duck presidents.

"I prefer to stand," said Bognor, directing his remark at his Queen, who stared graciously but unblinkingly back.

"As you wish," said Parkinson. "I'll be with you in just one minute."

The minute elapsed in a silence punctuated only by the scratch of the nib of Parkinson's pen across paper. At last he drew a thick, very straight line, cast the pen aside and looked up.

"Ah," he said.

Bognor was not going to help by volunteering some pleasantry. He said nothing at all.

"Something wrong, Bognor?"

"You could say that, yes."

"Care to tell me what it is?"

"I should hardly have thought that was necessary." Bognor thought his sarcasm sufficiently heavy for even Parkinson to catch.

"I shouldn't worry unduly," said Parkinson, spreading his mouth in what, had he been a humorous man, might have passed for a smile. "You may be under formal suspicion, but I scarcely think it's a suspicion which is going to be very seriously entertained."

Bognor frowned. He had no idea what Parkinson was talking about.

"I'm alluding to that . . . that person at my desk."

It was Parkinson's turn to frown and look fuddled. "Are you sure you won't sit?" he enquired. And on receiving the answer "no" said that, in that case, he would stand. When he heard this, Bognor, wishing to be difficult, said that in that case he would sit. The standing was making him giddy.

The charade completed, Parkinson said, "You mean Lingard?"

"Naturally."

"You've not met him before?"

"No, never."

"Pity. He's a good man. He may lack your, shall we say, individuality, Bognor, your unorthodox methodology, but he's eminently sound."

"I'd prefer it if he went back to Teddington."

"But Bognor . . ." Parkinson raised his eyes to the ceiling and pressed his palms together so tightly that his hands went white. "Don't you understand?"

"Perfectly." Bognor spoke crisply. "The second my back is turned you sneak some whippersnapper from Teddington into my office, plonk him down at my desk and don't even have the courtesy to tell me about it."

"On a point of fact, I sent you a memo about it last week. Foolish of me. I forgot that it's not your policy to read internal memoranda."

This was perfectly true. It was Bognor's practice to consign them to the waste-paper basket unperused. Just like bank statements and parking summonses. If it was important, he argued with some justice, he would find out soon enough by word of mouth. If it was not important it was just bumf and should be treated as such.

"What memo?"

For answer Parkinson stood up and walked over to the iron-grey filing cabinet, opened a drawer, pulled out a file and extracted a carbon copy of one of the departmental memos which sprayed forth from his desk like confetti. He handed it to Bognor. Bognor read.

"From H.O.O. (S.O.D.B.O.T.) to S. I. BOGNOR (S.O.D.B.O.T.) (C.C. & P)." This meant "From Head of Operations (Special Operations Department, Board of Trade) to Special Investigator Bognor (Special Operations Department, Board of Trade) (Codes, Ciphers and Protocol)." The message was succinct, but clear. "Re. Your persistent requests for transfer I am pleased to tell you that subject to availability, medical, interview, etc., etc., this has now gained approval. Your successor in this department will be S. I. Lingard of Teddington Branch who will be joining us on 18th inst. and to whom you are to give every assistance during the necessary period of transition."

"Of course." Bognor bit back the smile. "I'd quite forgotten today was the 18th inst. Silly me. By the way, how long exactly is the 'necessary period of transition' would you say?"

Parkinson gave virtually no indication that he was either sceptical or credulous regarding his subordinate's amnesia.

His eyes suggested amusement, but the rest of his expression was frankly frigid. "Could be a matter of weeks . . . or years. It depends."

"Depends on what?"

"Bognor, I have better things to do than discuss your dubious future, and there is the more immediate problem of the Master's murder. This man Mitten will be here in a matter of minutes, and I should like to think that we are properly prepared. So may we proceed?"

"Yes, of course." Bognor felt a little better now. He sat back in the regulation hard-backed, imitation-leather chair and smiled up at the Queen. She was beginning to go a little sepia at the edges. Almost time for a replacement.

"Now." Parkinson shuffled papers with the dexterity of the useful bridge player he was reputed to be. "This Mitten. We have nothing on file. What can you tell me?"

"He was my tutor. Well, one of my tutors."

"Not an absolutely wonderful recommendation." This time Parkinson *was* being humorous. Marginally.

Bognor took only mild umbrage. "Sixteenth-century English history is his speciality. Rise and fall of the gentry. Pre-Elizabethan, mainly. Knows more about Henry the Eighth than any man alive. He did the screenplay for that BBC series on *The Other Cromwell.*"

Parkinson scribbled. "Trustworthy?" he enquired, not looking up, "Sound? Liked? Respected?"

"Um," said Bognor, and hesitated. "Not entirely, but I couldn't put my finger on it."

"Have a teeny try." Parkinson smiled encouragingly. He was used to dealing with Bognor. You had to treat him like a boy of about twelve, he supposed, maybe thirteen. At least that was his experience. Occasionally he took you by surprise, but twelve or thirteen was usually about right. At least that was how he did treat him. It had never occurred to him to treat him like an adult. He doubted whether it would be very successful.

"There's something phoney about him," said Bognor,

obviously trying hard. "For example, he *is* the Honourable Waldegrave Mitten, but he's only the younger son of Ernest Mitten, the socialist food freak. Got a peerage from Attlee. Something to do with barracuda."

"Well?"

"Well, it doesn't, you know, make him the thirteenth son of the thirteenth earl or anything, but to see the way he dresses and the way he talks you'd think he was a Cecil or a Cavendish at the very least."

"Hmmm." Parkinson did some more scribbling.

"Married?"

"Divorced."

"Children?"

"Not that I've ever heard of."

Parkinson drummed on the desk with his fingers. "Popular sort of fellow is he? With his colleagues? With his students?"

"Quite," said Bognor, "but only quite. He works too hard at it. Too, you know, ingratiating. I suspect his pupils like him more than his colleagues."

"Does he have women?"

"He takes women out. Wines and dines them. Invites them to Glyndebourne and the Henley Regatta. But I'd be quite surprised if he beds them."

"What makes you say that?" Parkinson asked it sharply, genuine interest creeping into his voice for the first time during the interrogation.

"Instinct." Bognor regretted uttering the word as soon as it had issued forth.

"The trouble this department has had with that instinct of yours, Bognor." Parkinson was writing as he spoke. "Men have died for your instinct. You know that, don't you?"

"Up to a point."

Parkinson sucked his teeth. "Bit of a Bertie Wooftah, is that what you're trying to tell me. Eh? Is that it?"

"I wouldn't say that."

"Then what would you say?"

"Bit of a nothing. Sexually. But I think he's very concerned to suggest otherwise."

"No reason why he should have killed off the Master
himself?"

"Not that I can think of. No. None."

"Ambitious, is he?"

"Yes. Pretty."

"He'd fancy being the Master of Apocrypha, would he?"

Bognor considered this for a few moments. It had never
really occurred to him before.

"I'd think he'd prefer to have the respect of his peers,"
he ventured tentatively. "He's not taken very seriously as a
historian. Professional academics are childishly supercilious about colleagues who pander to popular taste. Particularly if they make a bundle out of some TV series."

"I thought *The Other Cromwell* was very fine" said
Parkinson tetchily. "So did Mrs. Parkinson. And she is
quite an authority. She has, I may say, read every one of
Lady Antonia Fraser's books. And her mother's."

Bognor did not know how to reply to this, but before he
was forced into something insupportably patronising he
was saved by the bell. Or, more accurately, the buzzer on
Parkinson's desk.

"Mr. Mitten and Ms. Frinton in reception for you, Mr.
Parkinson."

"Then be so good as to send them down." Parkinson
passed a hand over his scalp, while Bognor experienced a
disquieting lurch of the stomach which, unhappily, he
recognised as having something to do with emotional/
sexual anticipation.

"What's *she* doing with him?" he asked.

"Ah." Parkinson rubbed his hands together and smiled
in a mildly lascivious manner. "I understand you met her
the other night. She really is rather special."

Bognor felt his jaw betraying him. "How do you know I
met her the other night?"

"She told me. She's one of ours. In a manner of speaking."

"What manner of speaking?"

"Principally recruitment."

Bognor could no longer repress an expression of incredulity.

"Not all recruitments are as haphazard and indeed short-sighted as yours, I'm glad to say," said Parkinson. "Frinton isn't just recruiting for us, of course," he added. "She makes her assessments and pushes people in the direction of whichever branch of the security services she thinks most appropriate."

"Well!" said Bognor, "I've heard some preposterous things, but I *do* think employing the first woman Fellow of Apocrypha as a talent scout for Intelligence just about takes the biscuit."

"Your male chauvinism, if that's what it is, does you no credit," said Parkinson. "Frinton has done some superlative work in the field, quite apart from anything else. Her Hong Kong missions, especially, are classics of their kind."

But before Parkinson could expand on this extravagant claim, the two dons were ushered in. Mitten was in an ageing tweed suit, brown, well cut, with a canary pullover underneath and a woollen tie knotted loosely at the neck. Very much the outfit of a storybook Oxford don of the nineteen thirties. The J. B. Priestley look refined. Hermione Frinton was still in boots, above which she wore a long black skirt, a red waistcoat, herringbone tweed jacket and an enormously long silk scarf in the style of Isadora Duncan. Also a beret, very rakishly angled. She was smoking a Black Russian cigarette from a holder. She should have looked ridiculous. Instead she made Bognor, who like Parkinson was wearing regulation Board of Trade grey worsted, shiny at the elbows, and bagged at the knees, feel drab. Even Parkinson seemed impressed. His eyes glazed momentarily and he came out from behind his desk to make a big show of moving chairs around and ordering coffee.

Eventually they were all sitting as comfortably as the Civil Service furniture allowed, and Parkinson began by expressing his condolences. This did not take long and he moved briskly to business.

"I take it the police have been informed?"

Mitten replied. "Oh, yes indeed. We've played strictly according to the rules," he said, "straight bat to everything. Chief Inspector Chappie was round at bull's noon. Normally we don't let the police in college at all, but in the circumstances it seemed only proper."

"You were quite right Professor," said Parkinson, causing Mitten a moment's fleeting embarrassment. "And Chief Inspector Chappie is there right now, I take it?"

"Sorry." Mitten looked slightly more embarrassed this time, and Bognor caught Hermione Frinton's eye. She undoubtedly winked at him. "Figure of speech," continued Mitten. "I forget his name. Hermione?"

"Haven't a clue, darling. Couldn't have been Cuff, could it?"

"The name is hardly material," said Parkinson snappishly, then tried to redeem himself by flashing an ingratiating smile at Hermione. She did not smile back but flicked ash ostentatiously onto the carpet. A muscle in Parkinson's temple gave a scarcely perceptible twitch.

"Now as I understand it, this would be a perfectly conventional police investigation but for one or two unusual factors." Parkinson assumed his most magisterial professional tone. "The most significant of these is, of course, the identity of the deceased. This is bound to make the murder something of a *cause célèbre*. Then there is the matter of his position as Master and the circumstances surrounding the murder. Obviously you don't wish the good name of the college to be compromised in any way."

"There's been an Apocrypha College in Oxford for almost four hundred and fifty years," said Mitten, "and this is our first murder."

"Quite." Parkinson pursed his lips. "Now, from what you told me on the telephone Lord Beckenham died as the result of some foreign substance of an appropriately deadly nature being administered to him. Do we know what that was?"

"Faversham, our pathology Fellow, did tell me," said Mitten, "but I'm afraid it's slipped my mind."

"Arsenic?" suggested Hermione. "Strychnine? Paraquat?"

"No," said Mitten peevishly, "nothing like that. I do hope you're going to take this seriously, Dr. Frinton."

Hermione looked up at the ceiling and then made a play of removing the remains of her cigarette from its holder and stubbing it out on the heel of her boot.

"I don't think the name of the poison is of any more importance at this stage than the name of the Chief Inspector," said Parkinson, attempting to be placatory, "but, as I understand it, there is a strong suggestion that the dose may have been given while Lord Beckenham was drinking in your room. And among those present were you yourself, Professor Mitten, Dr. Frinton here, and you, Bognor."

"Yes," they said in unison.

"Which at this stage of the game," announced Parkinson, "makes all of you, in circumstantial terms, prime suspects."

There was a chorus, muted but unmistakeably one of dissent.

"At all events," went on Parkinson, "your presence on the last occasion the Master was seen alive is certainly enough to fuel speculation. If the Master was killed at your party, Professor, it's likely that those present are in for a sticky time."

"He wasn't killed at my party, Mr. Parkinson."

The atmosphere had suddenly grown unpleasant. Silence ensued.

"Aren't we rather jumping the gun?" asked Bognor eventually. He smiled round at the three lugubrious faces. "Waldegrave hasn't explained why he's here at all. I mean, I can see that it's a bit of an embarrassment all round, but despite Lord Beckenham's fleeting association with the Board of Trade in the dim and distant past, it's scarcely our pigeon. As you said, it's a straightforward matter for CID, Oxford."

"I don't think," said Mitten, "that it's going to be in the least straightforward. There was very little straightforward about the Master while he was alive and I see no reason to think that there will be anything straightforward about him now that he's dead. And you ought to know, in any case, that there is nothing whatever that is likely to prove straightforward about a murder investigation in Apocrypha."

Parkinson sighed. "The point is," he said heavily, "that you at Apocrypha"—and here he nodded at Mitten—"are anxious to solve this matter with the minimum fuss, annoyance, publicity, inconvenience, call it what you will . . ."

Mitten nodded.

"And to make this possible, notice I say possible"—and here he glared meaningfully at Bognor—"to make this possible you have negotiated an understanding with the local constabulary under the terms of which the investigation can be kept, at least partly—how shall I put it?—in the family. To whit, you have proposed that since there are two professionals involved already, their involvement should be put onto a basis which has proper authority."

"You mean," said Bognor very slowly, "that you have persuaded the Oxford police to work with myself and Hermione . . . Dr. Frinton?"

"Spot on," said Mitten eagerly.

"Oh." Bognor oozed unhappiness, not to say disbelief.

"As far as Dr. Frinton is concerned," said Parkinson, "I can only say that it's a most sagacious decision, and I dare say that unravelling the secret intricacies of Chinese secret societies will prove markedly similar to doing the same thing in the Senior Common Room."

"Ha, ha," interjected Mitten, causing Parkinson to blink, but scarcely to pause. "As for yourself, Bognor, I can only say that I share your incredulity. But far be it from me to stand in the way of town and gown. All I ask is that this time you somehow contrive to organise things in an orderly and methodical and unobtrusive manner which, for once, reflects no discredit on this department."

"No problem," said Bognor.

CHAPTER 2

"It really is rather bloody." Bognor thrust a piece of roll into the garlic butter left behind by his dozen escargots and watched it soak in like bath water entering a loofah.

His wife pushed a sliver of gherkin to the side of her plate.

"In what way bloody?"

"The presumption." He put the bread in his mouth. "Strange men from Teddington sitting at my desk without so much as a by-your-leave. One's old tutor clicking his fingers and making you come running, just as if he was ordering up your weekly essay. Do this. Do that. I'm too old to be treated like an errant infant."

"One's never too old for that." Monica drank a little Gewürtztraminer. This was a farewell dinner. He was leaving for Oxford first thing next morning. He would not be allowed home till the murder was solved. No one knew when that would be, but it would take time. Monica had announced her intention of trying out that restaurant on the Banbury Road, new since their day, about which one heard such mixed reports.

"Do they really think it was one of you?" she asked.

"I don't think they seriously imagine it was me. Not seriously." Bognor dipped bread again and pulled a face. "Not that that will stop boring Parkinson making an unending heavy joke out of it. And I don't think anyone seriously suspects Hermione Frinton. Mitten, well probably not. From what Parkinson let drop I sense that he thinks Mitten coveted the Mastership and knocked the old man off in order to get it."

"Is that likely?"

"*I* don't think so. But who am I to cast doubt on a pet theory belonging to Parkinson? You know Mitten."

"Yes," admitted Monica. "Don't like much, either."

"No, but that doesn't make him a murderer."

"Granted." She leaned back in her chair to allow the waiter to remove her plate. "But supposing he really did want to be Master of Apocrypha, this was his best chance."

"How do you mean?"

"If there was an ordinary election, which there was going to be in about a year's time, he wouldn't have an earthly."

"Probably not."

"But if he was suddenly thrown into the Mastership by a piece of luck like this, he would have a few months to show how well he could do the job and he could go into an election as a strong internal candidate. And as acting Master he'd have a lot of say in how the election was organised."

Not at Balliol

"It's conceivable."

The waiter returned, bearing the rack of lamb they were to share. The wine waiter followed behind with a bottle of Hermitage. There was a natural break in conversation.

"Not a strong-enough motive," said Bognor. "Mitten wants all sorts of things out of life, but the Mastership isn't one of them."

"I wouldn't be so sure." Monica smiled at him. "What about you?"

"What about me?"

"Did you do it?"

"What do you mean?"

Monica brushed a stray strand of hair from her eyes.

"You heard. Did you do it?" Then she giggled. "Oh, all right," she said, "*I* know you didn't do it, but Chief Inspector Chappie doesn't know."

"Smith," said Bognor irritably. "His name's Smith. How's your lamb?"

"Fine. All right then—Smith. He may decide you did it. You obviously had an opportunity, what about motive?"

Bognor reluctantly decided to enter into the spirit of the game. After all, she was his wife. He was fond of her. He would not be seeing her until the weekend.

"No motive that I can think of. I liked the old boy."

"Not good enough. You can kill the thing you love. You know that."

"I didn't love him. Just liked him. Quite."

"That's better." She lowered her eyelids and then looked up at him from under the lashes, mischievously. An old trick, but Bognor still enjoyed the mannerism. "I can think of a motive."

"Don't be ridiculous." He wiped his mouth with a napkin and drank. "I think this is a silly game."

"It's not a game, darling. It's real. The old man is dead. And even though it may seem preposterous, you could be considered a suspect. Especially by some resentful flatfoot from the Oxford City police station. Remember how they dislike the University. One of them tried to rape me that night when I was climbing out of your room."

"Oh, rubbish," he exclaimed, "he was just helping you down and you lost your grip."

"You don't know the half of it. He pestered me for weeks after that."

"You led him on. I bet you did."

"Shut up, and listen, Simon Bognor!" She wagged her fork at him. "Now. Why was this man Lingard in your office this morning?"

"Don't remind me of him." Bognor had not thought of the interloper since dinner began. The mention of his name induced definite palpitations. "Oily little creep. He was up just after me. Trinity man. Typical. Stowe and Trinity. He reeked of after-shave."

"He was there because you've applied for a transfer,

Simon. And your applications are to the Treasury, the Foreign Office and the Home Office."

"So?"

"They all involve promotion."

"Arguably."

"And they're politically sensitive. Or likely to be."

"I doubt. Anyway the Board of Trade is politically sensitive."

"Well"—she paused to chew—"my point is that before anything like that came through there would have to be a whole cat's-cradle of red tape and paperwork. References taken up, opinions sought. Meetings, soundings, interviews."

"I'm sorry"—Bognor picked up a bone in his fingers and gnawed at it speculatively—"I'm absolutely adrift. No idea what on earth you're on about."

"My point is that the one place they're bound to go back to, to discover any character flaws, political defects and general bad-lottery is Apocrypha. The Jesuits are always supposed to have said that if they had a child until the age of seven or whatever, then they had its soul, but that's manifestly not so. It's what happens at University that matters. That's when Burgess became Burgess, Maclean, Maclean, and Blunt, Blunt."

"That was Cambridge. And before my time."

"You're being deliberately silly. You know how slowly the Civil Service moves. I'm quite certain the first thing that they'd do before moving you to the FO or the Treasury would be to get on to Beckenham and ask him to turn up your file."

"They'd ask Parkinson for his file first."

"Possibly. But your University file would be a jolly close first."

"So you think I killed Lord Beckenham to stop him telling the Treasury snoopers about the time I was sick on staircase nine or planted daffodils in Trinity Junior Common Room."

"You know what I mean, Simon," she said. "I'm being quite serious."

"*Quite* serious," he mimicked her. "I know you are, darling, and I see what you're getting at."

She set her knife and fork neatly together and wiped her mouth fastidiously. "You do and you don't," she said. "I'm really only using you as an illustration. What I'm saying is that if an old Apocrypha man was in for a job, then the people who are considering him for it would be idiotic if they didn't run a rule over Apocrypha. And my hunch is that if there was any dirt available the Master would be most likely to have it. So it is at least conceivable that one of your whizzy contemporaries wanted to shut him up before he could spill the beans about the skeletons in his cupboard."

"You mix your metaphors wonderfully," he teased, "but I do see your point. And I take it, too. Jolly shrewd." He put out his hand and patted hers affectionately as it lay on the table between them.

"Don't be so patronising," she protested. "What was he drinking?"

"Same as he always drank. That hideous raspberry liqueur he always took after dinner."

"Framboise?"

"No, worse than that. Don't know what it was called or where it came from. Polish, I think. Very strong. People he knew used to keep a bottle in their rooms specially in case he just blew in unannounced. Never known to drink anything else."

"So whoever did it need only have doctored the bottle, not just the glass."

"I suppose. That should be perfectly easy to prove. And now can we talk about something else? I'm finding this distinctly morbid. How was your lamb?"

He returned to Oxford by train since Monica insisted she needed the car. She was helping Fiona out at the art gallery. At least Bognor thought that was what she was doing. Or maybe she was helping Camilla out in her boutique in Camden Passage. Or was she typing and answering the phone for Richard because Vivien was off sick? Or for Vivien because Richard was off sick? He did wish, now that they were married, that she would complete the act of settling down and find herself a permanent job. He simply couldn't keep up with her peripatetic universal jill-of-all-trades acts. No no, it was none of these things, he realised guiltily; she was helping Myrtle provide a buffet for a hundred and twenty Darby and Joans because she, Myrtle, had rashly agreed to bail out Caroline, who had got lumbered with organising some "do" for her pet charity. How much less complicated and wearing it was to be a mere special investigator with the Board of Trade, even if it did mean that he had to go by train because Monica needed the car. He didn't like the car anyway, which was a new Mini Metro, purchased in an excess of patriotic enthusiasm to postpone the inevitable collapse of the British Motor Industry. What was the country coming to, he wondered morosely, as he bought a *Times* and a *Telegraph* at the Paddington Station bookstall. Even the distinguished old Masters of Oxford Colleges were not allowed to fade away in peace but were foully done to death by over-ambitious Trinity men from Teddington only concerned with their own careers. Made you despair.

"Penny for them?" said a slightly husky voice, trained on his left ear and coming from alarmingly close range. He gave a start, glanced guiltily up and found himself confronted by the disconcertingly flared nostrils of Dr. Hermione Frinton.

"*Quelle* coincidence," she said. "I'm sorry. I didn't mean to frighten you. As a matter of fact, that was the third question I've addressed to you. You all right?"

"Perfectly," he replied stuffily. "Just thinking. That's all."

"Very preoccupying—thought," she said. "I hadn't put you down as one of the great thinkers, somehow."

"And what *had* you put me down as, exactly?"

"That would be telling, wouldn't it." She laughed throatily, causing Bognor an uneasy tremor of incipient desire. She was no longer in yesterday's skirt, but instead had reverted to the tight trousers which did the maximum possible for her elongated legs. She also, in a phrase he associated with his old friend Sir Erris Beg, was a "fine mover." Bognor sensed trouble ahead. He adored his wife, but he was uneasily mindful of the fact that a prime reason for their marriage was that he found the idea of being unfaithful to a wife somehow more acceptable than being unfaithful to a mistress or "live-in girl friend," as the displeasing contemporary argot preferred. Not that he had ever been unfaithful, though there had been some near misses.

They were walking towards the platform. He offered to carry her bag, which was an expensive light-tan leather creation with gold initials and a number of tags, among which he noticed those of the Eastern and Oriental in Penang, the Hong Kong Mandarin, and Las Brisas in Acapulco.

"I hardly imagine you were delivering a paper on *Beowulf* in Acapulco," he tried, banteringly he thought, and not altogether unwittily.

"Hmmm." She smiled down at him, as if to say, "Funny little man." Bognor shrank but persevered.

"Nor Penang."

"No," she said. "Though, in point of fact, the British Council did arrange for me to give a talk on Shakespearean metaphor."

"And did you?"

"No. I gave them 'Maugham to Burgess and Theroux: Anglo-Saxon Attitudes to the Peninsular: Studies in Literary Imperialism.' Maugham's a speciality of mine. Would you believe I read them 'The Hairless Mexican' in Acapulco, standing naked on the seashore?"

"No."

"Hmmm," she said again, giving him another of her patronising looks. "Are we going first?" she asked as they passed along the platform.

"Parkinson doesn't like it," said Bognor. "He's on a permanent economy drive."

"He looks as if he's its original victim," she said. "Breakfast then?"

"I've had breakfast."

"Have another. Nothing succeeds like excess. You must know that."

"I'll have a coffee."

"You do just that."

The dining car was virtually empty, British Rail meals being beyond the means of most of those who travelled the Oxford line, and they easily found a table for two.

"Well," she purred, when they had settled themselves and the train began to ease out of the station, "isn't this fun?"

"Yes," he said.

"I've wanted to meet you for ages. I've been a great fan, ever since that business at Beaubridge Friary. I read the files. *Very* imaginative."

"Thank you."

"It never occurred to me that one day we'd actually be working together."

"No." Bognor was feeling rather nonplussed.

"Ciggy?" She waved a pack of Black Russian at him.

He declined. He would like to ask if she was really a tutor in English as well as being in the employ of the Intelligence Services but judged this to be unwise. Instead he said, "Which College were you in? As an undergraduate."

"LMH," she said. Clearly she read his thoughts, for she went on: "I'm quite genuine. The teeniest little bit after your time . . . but I did get one of the best firsts of my year, not to mention a quarter blue for basketball. It is said that I slept my way through the whole of All Souls'." She exhaled smoke and said, in the manner of Lady Bracknell, "But that is a lie."

She was having the continental breakfast. Her orange juice arrived. So did the coffee, at least two thirds of which was still in the cup. Bognor poured his saucer off, clumsily, as they rattled over some bumpy points just outside Ealing Broadway.

"What's this chap Smith like?" he asked.

For a moment she looked blank, then she grinned. "You mean our Inspector Chappie." She sipped her orange juice and laughed. "Fearful halitosis and that fatal combination of egg and chip."

"Egg and chip?"

"Outsize ego, chip on shoulder. They seldom go together but when they do it's cop-out time. However, he will have to do as he is told. He has rather delicious ears. Distinctly edible except that it would be impossible to get within range on account of the breath." She gazed at him in an appraising manner. "Your ears could hardly be said to be your best point, but you have the sweetest nose. I do hope we're going to be friends."

This is ridiculous, thought Bognor. Who on earth does she think she is playing at? Out loud he said, "So do I." And then in his most serious voice: "How long have you been . . . er . . . one of ours?"

"Since I came down. Lord Beckenham recruited me personally."

Bognor choked on his coffee. "*Who* recruited you personally?"

She fluttered her eyelashes. They had to be false. They reminded him of caterpillars. "Becky. Your old Master. He was one of ours too. Didn't you know?"

"No. I did not."

She eyed him suspiciously. "No," she said at last, "I do believe you didn't. I'm his replacement. In a manner of speaking. That's part of the point."

"I see." He dabbed at the coffee on the tabletop, not

daring to look up. Eventually he said, "In what sense was he 'one of ours'?"

"Oh, not much more than the University rep really. He co-ordinated intelligence on people like the exchange students and the Rhodes Scholars, supervised selection, helped with the files on subversives. Routine stuff. No field work, needless to say. He wasn't what you'd call a real pro like you and me. Last of the old school in a way."

"How many people knew?"

"Enough."

"Parkinson, for instance?"

"Probably not." She shrugged. "I'm afraid that with the spectacular exception of your own irruptions into the world of espionage, intrigue, chicanery and international whatsit, the Board of Trade hardly features in the divine order of things. Not even Special Operations Division. It's desperately run-of-the-mill, other-rank stuff."

"Someone once said 'all cloak and no dagger,'" said Bognor, wondering half-heartedly if it had been himself but not wishing, in present company, to take credit for the aphorism. Just in case.

"Quite." She leaned forward in a confidential manner, and Bognor was disturbingly aware of breasts, concealed though they were under an exotic poncho-style garment of probably foreign extraction. Also of her scent, which was expensive and, in a way he was unable to identify, suggestive, even rude.

"Chief Inspector Chappie doesn't know," she stage-whispered, "nor Waldegrave. Nor should they. Also, I'm determined that the post-mortem results should be hushed up for as long as possible."

"You'll be lucky," he said. Bognor had a low opinion of pathologists, coroners and policemen. Hushing things up was not, in his experience, their style at all.

The train had hurried through Slough and was approaching Maidenhead. Dr. Frinton was eating toast, heavily buttered and marmaladed. It was clear she did not have to worry about her figure. Before long they would reach Reading and turn north along the Thames Valley, one of Bognor's favourite railway journeys.

"We must still try," she said. A ticket collector hove in sight and demanded tickets. Hermione frowned heavily at Bognor to indicate that even ticket collectors have ears and said very loudly, "Super day!"

"Super," he agreed.

When the official had passed along and a similar charade had been enacted for the benefit of the attendant with the coffee-pot, Bognor, catching his colleague's theatricality, whispered hoarsely, "Do you have any theories?"

Before answering, she stood up on the pretext of adjusting her clothing and peered about her. There was no one in the table alongside them on the other side of the aisle. Behind Bognor a bald clergyman with a hearing aid and a frumpish wife were reading newspapers. Behind Hermione there was a scattering of businessmen, mainly English with American and Japanese companions, some of whom could have been tourists.

"Not here," she announced firmly and with finality. "We'd better talk properly at my place. Where are you staying?"

Bognor was at a loss to understand why she had been so indiscreet about the dead Master and was now being so tight-lipped about her theories. He guessed she had none and was going to spend the rest of the journey making some up. If you were to ask him, he would have said she was a fraud. An alluring fraud. Positive Mata Hari, in fact. But a fraud.

"The Randolph." He liked the Randolph. It had been tarted up since his undergraduate days, but at least it survived, unlike the Mitre, which had been turned into a steak house.

"Silly billy, you could have stayed *chez moi.*"

"People would have talked. My wife most of all."

"I didn't know you were married."

"Oh."

She looked into his eyes until he dropped his gaze. Then she chuckled.

"My place is in Walton Street. Just round the corner from the Randolph. We'll make it campaign HQ. Now. Tell me about your wife. Is she *madly* in love with you?"

They did not talk about the murder again on the train. Nor did they discuss Monica. Bognor never discussed Monica with anybody but Monica. He was old-fashioned enough to find it indelicate. For almost half an hour they talked about landscapes in literature. This seemed a safe subject and one on which there was a measure of mutual agreement. At Oxford station Bognor carried Hermione's bag through the murky tunnel which ran under the railway line. Then they shared a taxi, it being far too far to walk. Bognor dropped her off at her flat in Walton Street.

"Ta-ta, then," she said, stretching those legs. "Shan't kiss you good-bye in case people talk. See you in half an hour."

Bognor mumbled something incomprehensible and wondered what was happening to him. He felt that he was being swept along by a force that belonged to nature rather than any human agency, and as he collected his key in the foyer of the Randolph, much smarter now, but still with that familiar atmosphere of converted aeroplane hangar, he felt glum. He was glummer still to find a message from Chief Inspector Chappie. "Must stop calling him that," he said out loud to himself as he skimmed through the note, scrawled in semi-legible pencil.

Smith had been to the hotel half an hour earlier and was calling again in about twenty minutes. Bognor sighed. He had been anticipating his business meeting with Hermione with an odd and guilty mixture of despair and eagerness. She had given him her number for emergencies like this. He rang to tell her the bad news.

38 A *Small Masterpiece*

"Best get it over with," she said. "Then potter round here and I'll have a large G and T waiting to take away the taste."

"Anything you'd advise me to say?"

"As little as possible, darling. See you soon. Have fun."

He sank onto the forbidding-looking single bed. He hoped he was going to be able to stand the pace. Still, having her flat as a refuge was a blessing. He could never understand why enormous reception rooms in hotels so often denoted tiny bedrooms and vice versa. You couldn't swing a mouse in this glorified cupboard, let alone a cat. He would have to get something bigger for the weekend when Monica came. There wasn't even a view—just some roof and guttering. Some of the rooms must have views across to the Ashmolean. The Ashmolean was a view worth having. This emphatically wasn't. The phone rang. Oh well, he thought, better get it over with. He counted three, then picked it up and said in his briskest, most official, most efficient manner: "Bognor, Board of Trade."

"Oh, Simon, thank heaven I've found you. I've got to talk to you."

"Who is this?" It hardly sounded like an Oxford city policeman. Far too familiar, and also far too grand and well educated. A gown rather than a town voice.

"Oh, sorry. It's Sebastian Vole here, Simon. I hope you don't mind my ringing you at your hotel. Waldy Mitten told me I'd probably get you at the Randolph. Hope you haven't got one of the maid's rooms up in the attic. Look, actually, something pretty urgent's cropped up and I wondered if we could have a spot of lunch. Waldy's genned me up, as a matter of fact. He thought it best, and in the circs, I'm bound to say I'm glad he did."

Bognor swore under his breath. Another postponement of his business meeting with Hermione. And why had the preposterous Mitten unburdened himself to Vole? "You sound very agitated, Sebastian. Calm down and speak slowly. Whatever is it?"

"I *am* very agitated, actually," said Vole. "I hadn't realised until this morning that the Master didn't die of a stroke or a heart attack or indigestion or whatever. Someone else did it. And you're investigating."

"Look, Sebastian"—Bognor tried to keep the impatience out of his voice—"it is very distressing. I'm touched by your distress, which I share myself. Now do you simply wish to communicate this to me, or do you have something new to contribute?" He sounded like Parkinson, a conscious parody.

"Oh, it's new all right," said Vole. "Dynamite. It'll singe your eyebrows."

Bognor did not want his eyebrows singed, but he did not say so.

"Very well," he said flatly, "lunch then. Where do you want to meet?"

"Turf?"

"Not exactly discreet."

"I suppose not," said Vole, "but we can meet there and move on. Maybe go for a walk."

"O.K." He looked at his watch. "Shall we say twelve-thirty?"

"Twelve-thirty it is."

He hung up and immediately phoned Hermione Frinton again. She sounded gratifyingly disappointed.

"Never mind," she said. "Business before business. I'll put your G and T on ice. Come and get it as soon as you're free. And don't believe too much of what Vole tells you. He's inclined to exaggerate, and my historian friends tell me his reputation is wildly inflated."

"I wasn't aware he had a reputation," remarked Bognor.

"That's what I mean." She laughed. "See you soon."

Actually, this exchange was unfair to Vole, and Bognor knew it. Soon after leaving Oxford, he had produced a slim volume on Italian Fascism, entitled *Mussolini: Mannerism Maketh Man*, which was generally considered the cleverest book on its subject for years. It was, however, a

young man's book: flashy and as meretricious as its title
suggested. The most venerated authority on the subject,
old Cormorant of All Souls', had blown Vole out of the
academic water over an entire *Times Literary Supplement*
front. As a result Vole had resolved to produce nothing
else in a hurry, except for the occasional review and
learned paper. For more than fifteen years he had been en-
gaged on a magnum opus, the exact subject of which was
known only to Vole, Mrs. Vole and his loyal secretary *cum*
researcher. Its publication was annually awaited, and had
been for almost a decade. The saga had now gone on so
long that it could truthfully be said that Vole's very life, or
at least his career, depended on it. Privately Bognor did
not believe that Vole would have the guts to publish during his lifetime.

He had just hung up his spare grey suit, even more
shiny and bagged than the one he was wearing, when the
phone shrilled again. This time it *was* Smith alias Chappie. He was downstairs. Bognor descended with a heavy
heart to find a short stout individual in a regulation CID
fawn mackintosh and a pork-pie hat, which he had not removed.

"Well, well, well," said this person, taking Bognor's
right hand in both of his and squeezing uncomfortably
hard, "long time no see. Don't suppose you remember
me?"

Not for the first time in his life Bognor had an over-
whelming desire to return home at once.

"Must be twenty years ago if it's a day," said the policeman, relinquishing Bognor's hand and stepping back to
appraise him. "You've changed. I'll say that."

"Sorry," said Bognor. "I don't have any recollection."

"How about a coffee?" enquired the Inspector, not waiting for an answer but leading the way briskly towards the
lounge. "I said to the missus when I heard, I said, 'Well,
that's a turn up for the book and no mistake.' 'Course, I
said, 'He won't remember!' "

"I give in," conceded Bognor, wearily subsiding into a chintz armchair. "Give me a clue."

"Give you a clue, eh?" Smith scratched his chin and screwed up his eyes. After some cogitation he said, "About two o'clock in the morning. Cold night. I was on duty, walking past the back gate of Apocrypha College and what do I see emerging from a first-floor window but a pair of legs, female. Shapely, too, as far as one could judge from the lamplight."

"Ah." A Cheshire cat expression, fatuous, beatific but comprehending, illuminated Bognor's face. "Are you telling me it was you, who . . ."

"Assisted you and your lady friend out of a tight corner. Right in one."

"What an extraordinary coincidence!" Bognor was almost cheered by it. He ordered their coffee with something approaching enthusiasm.

"Small world, innit?" The Inspector pulled out a packet of filter-tip cigarettes, offered one to Bognor—who declined—lit, and puffed. "'Course I transferred a little while afterwards to CID. And here we are. Who'd have thought it? She was a bit of all right, your bird, if I remember correctly. On the big side. Well built, if you follow."

"Funny," said Bognor, "I'd forgotten all about it. Or had, until my wife reminded me about it the other day."

"Wife? What. Same bird? Married her, did you?"

"Yes."

"Well, well. Good for you. Don't mind admitting I wouldn't have minded a spot of dalliance if it hadn't been for . . . Well, it's a long time ago."

Bognor toyed with the idea of telling Smith that Monica had called him a rapist, but decided against it. She always exaggerated. Besides, one sneeze from her and this little man would have blown away. Out loud he said, "Clever of you to remember after all these years."

Smith glowed. "Like I say, she was a bit of all right, your, er, missus, if you'll pardon the expression. And I never for-

get a name. Monica Becket and Simon Bognor. That's a
name and a half, eh, Bognor? Never come across another.
Twenty-three years on the force and never known another
Bognor. Met a couple of Worthings and a Deal, and Vis-
count Weymouth of course, but never another Bognor.
Odd, innit?"

"And now you've got a Frinton to add to your list."

"Yeah." The Inspector stubbed his cigarette out very deliberately. "Bit of all right, she is. Big girl like Mrs. Bognor. But too much of an intellectual for my liking. Not altogether straight. Still, you can't fault her legs."

"No," Bognor agreed. He wasn't sure he didn't also
agree with his colleague's character assessment, but he
judged it better not to say so. Their coffee arrived. Bognor
was mother. The Inspector took his milky with three
sugars.

"Well," said Bognor, a shift of tone indicating that the
time had come to cease frivolous small talk and move to
the agenda. Also, that he was not only mother but chairman too. "What progress have you made?"

"I'll be quite candid," announced Smith, "and the fact
is, we've made very little progress at all."

"I see." Bognor examined his fingertips and waited.

"Fact is, Simon." He paused. "Don't mind if I call you
Simon, do you?" Bognor shook his head to convey that the
familiarity was perfectly in order, if not wholly desirable.
"Fact is, present company excepted, it's never easy dealing
with the college people."

"I can imagine." He could, too. Only too well.

"Frankly, I'm out of my depth. So I'd value your cooper-
ation. I would, really."

"You shall have it." Bognor was as susceptible to flattery
as the next man. Perhaps more so, since he was so seldom
accorded it.

"You must have discovered something?" he prompted.

"Right." The Inspector drew breath. "One. The deceased was poisoned. I've got a name for the stuff back at the office. Our experts say it acts in about an hour."

"And the time of death?"

"About three."

"And he was drinking in Mitten's rooms until about a quarter to."

"So I understand."

"Could it have been self-administered?"

"No trace of a supply in the Master's Lodgings. No sign of any suicide note. No evidence of depression. I'm inclined to rule that one out. Until we find something to prove otherwise."

same as Mane as B.

"His wife had died." Bognor remembered Lady Mabel well. Small, pear-shaped, nearly always smiling, she had never ironed out her northern accent, as her husband had done. She was an unusual Master's wife. Very few airs and graces. He'd no idea how she and her husband had got on together. Well enough, as far as could be seen. Nothing spectacular. Certainly nothing to suggest that Lord Beckenham would be so grief-stricken at her passing that he would commit suicide.

"That was three years ago," said the Inspector. "Let's forget the idea he killed himself."

"All right," said Bognor. "Method. I suppose someone spiked his drink."

"Looks like a Mickey Finn," agreed Smith. "Had a bit of luck there."

"Oh?"

"Post-mortem was done unusually fast, right?"

"Yes."

"Don't ask me why. I think it's partly a question of Mitten and his friends pulling rank. Showing they can cut through the red tape."

"That follows."

"Result of that is that we know it's murder before Monday morning. And Mr. Mitten's scout doesn't come in till

Monday morning, so the glasses haven't been washed up."
He paused. "So we've had them removed for analysis."

"Very good," said Bognor. "Which will demonstrate
conclusively that his drink was fixed."

"I hope so. And that proves that he was done in by one
of the people drinking with him in Mitten's rooms, doesn't
it."

"Not necessarily," said Bognor. "The Master always
drank a peculiar sort of Polish raspberry fire-water. No one
else ever touched the stuff. Doctoring that would have
been a surefire way of getting him."

"Sound thinking," said Smith.

"Not mine. That's Mrs. Bognor's theory."

Smith raised his eyebrows. "She in this line of country
too?"

"Not officially, no, but she is an ever-constant help in
time of trouble."

"Not just a pretty face?"

"No. Definitely not."

The Inspector lit another cigarette and drew on it, then
breathed out, watching the smoke as if it might have some
message for him.

"On the assumption," he said, as the smoke drifted
away across the lounge, "that the Master's drink—his glass,
not the bottle—was fixed during your late-night session
after dinner. Who could have done it? And how?"

Bognor closed his eyes and tried to visualise the scene. It
was surprisingly easy. Old Beckenham in his equally an-
cient dinner jacket, literally green with age, the edge of his
bulging waistcoat showing broken stitching, the shoes
split. Mitten in his tobacco-brown smoking jacket; Hermione in that clinging backless black number. Vole pinkly
chubby. Edgware so very neat, everything creased razor-
sharp, including the parting of his hair. Rook fleshily expensive with heavy gold cuff-links and matching studs in
his old-fashioned boiled shirt. Crutwell smoking a pipe—
Mr. Avuncular Housemaster himself.

"We were all a bit pissed," he said, opening his eyes. "In fact, to be quite honest, at breakfast on Sunday morning the others claimed I'd said several things of which I had no recollection whatever." He laughed a hollow laugh. Inspector Smith, for once, did not join in. Bognor coughed. "Well, as you've probably seen, Mitten's rooms consist of that little entrance hall where he has the elephant's-foot umbrella stand and the coat hooks. Then there's the dining room. Then the drawing room/study and then the bedroom leading off that. The drinks are in a corner cupboard in the dining room."

"And you were all in the drawing room?"

"Yes."

"Doors shut?"

Bognor closed his eyes again and concentrated. "Most of the time, yes. I seem to remember someone protesting about the draught. But there was a lot of to-ing and fro-ing."

"Did Mitten help you to drinks, or did you help yourselves?"

"He gave us our first ones. After that we just helped ourselves. Quite a lot. Hence all the to-ing and fro-ing." Bognor was beginning to feel uncomfortable. He knew he was not under suspicion. Not really. And yet this felt like a proper interrogation.

"What were you drinking?"

"What, me personally?"

"Yes, you personally."

"Cognac. Brandy. Hine." He drank some more coffee and noticed that the palm of his right hand was sweaty. He hoped it was just the central heating.

"And after the first drink, which was handed to you by Mitten, you helped yourself?"

"Yes."

"Several times?"

"'Fraid so. Yes, several times."

"And when you helped yourself, did you help anyone else?"

Bognor's face contorted itself with the effort of remembering through the fog of alcohol and cigar.

"I think so," he said at last. "As far as I can remember whenever anyone went to get another drink they sort of looked round to see if anyone else wanted a refill and took an extra glass or two with them. But it was all pretty chaotic."

"So at one time or another everybody left the room to get drink?" The little man was leaning forward, his breath quickening. His face had lost much of its roundness and had developed unsuspected sharp edges, so that it was almost ferrety. Bognor began to wonder if he was quite the oaf he appeared to be on first acquaintance.

"Not Lord Beckenham. He remained rooted to his chair throughout. Threatening to go pop at any moment."

Smith raised an interlocutory eyebrow. Bognor emitted a cracked humourless chuckle. "Figure of speech," he apologised, "unfortunate choice of phrase."

"No, not at all. Very apt. Very apt indeed." Smith's eyes were very black. They were screwed up now. Bognor was reminded of raisins in a steamed pudding.

"Otherwise everybody went out, except for Hermione Frinton."

"Male gallantry survives in Apocrypha, eh?"

"I suppose so." Bognor was feeling most discomfited. "I seem to remember a certain amount of badinage about Germaine Greerism and whether a female Fellow could be one of the chaps. That sort of thing."

Smith's expression indicated that he saw nothing humorous in this. It also implied that such childishness was only to be expected.

"Was everyone drinking brandy?"

"As I said, the Master was drinking his raspberry tipple. Some of the rest of us were on brandy, some on Scotch."

"Scotch with water?"

"I suppose so. Yes." Bognor racked his brains feverishly. A piece of scum from the top of his coffee had attached itself in a thin film to the bottom of one of Smith's two front fangs. Bognor was becoming mesmerised by it. He felt like a rabbit trapped by a car's headlight. "Why am I reacting like this?" he asked himself nervously. "I'm totally innocent and yet this man is going to make me confess to something in a minute. He's eerie."

"Where did the water come from?"

"Um," said Bognor desperately, "water?"

"For the Scotch," prompted Inspector Smith.

"Oh. From a jug." He scratched his thinning hair. "No, no. I tell a lie. No jug, no jug. Some people went out to the scout's pantry on the landing where there was a sink. And some people went into Waldy Mitten's bedroom and filled their glasses from his wash-basin."

Inspector Smith nodded sagely.

"Scout's pantry?" he repeated.

"Scout's pantry. Sort of servant's kitchenette."

"But no scout?"

"Not that I could see."

"But he'd have served at dinner?"

"Probably."

Smith pulled out a shorthand notebook and made a scribbled entry in pencil. "I'll have to talk to him," he said, "and I'm going to have to talk to the others. Mitten and Frinton I've spoken to already. Frinton's in the clear, I suppose, being one of ours. In a manner of speaking." He sniggered mirthlessly. "No reason not to suspect Mitten. Bit of a pooftah, is he?"

"I don't think so. Everyone seems to think that. My guess is he's sexless."

"Never made a pass at you then, did he. Eh?" Smith sniggered again. Bognor felt this was more like Chief Inspector Chappie.

"No, never, I'm pleased to say."

"Obviously knew your attentions were otherwise en-gaged, eh? With the future Mrs. Bognor, eh?" For a hideous moment Bognor was sure that the diminutive detective was going to say, "Nudge, nudge, know what I mean?" in the manner of the man in the Monty Python sketch, but mercifully, he simply put his notebook away and licked his lips in a tentative fashion, succeeding, incidentally, in removing the coffee stain from his tooth. "And then we have Messrs. Edgware, Vole, Rook and Crutwell," he said. "What about them?"

"Well." Bognor looked at his watch. "As a matter of fact, I've got a rendezvous with Sebastian Vole in ten minutes' time at the Turf. Can we adjourn this till a bit later?"

"Certainly, Simon. Only too glad. I've set up a little incident room in the college. The Old Shakespeare Room."

"Yes. I remember it. The college's most famous alumnus."

"Really?" The Inspector seemed surprised. "I had no idea that Shakespeare was an Oxford man."

"No," said Bognor, "nor have most people."

CHAPTER 3

He was late for his meeting with Vole. It was twelve forty-five by the time he had shaken off the policeman, relieved himself at the Randolph urinal, and ambled along the Broad, pausing to inspect the books in the window of Blackwells and marvel at the papier-mâché hideousness of the new emperor's heads outside the Sheldonian. ("Beer-bohm would have *hated* you!" he called out in disgust, causing several human heads to turn.) He hurried down the absurdly narrow alley which led to the pub and burst in to find Vole sitting at the bar with a neat Scotch and a pint of Guinness in front of him. Also the *Times*, folded in four with the crossword uppermost.

"Ah, Simon," he said, "five, three, seven. What don had to change in mistake for 'sensational'?"

"Don't be ridiculous, Sebastian. You know perfectly well I can't understand the crossword. Monica's the crossword queen."

"Quite right. Let's ring her up. This is driving me crazy." Vole spoke sorrowfully. "What'll you have?" he asked.

Bognor opted for a Guinness but no Scotch.

"Well then, what's all this?" he asked brusquely. "I'm very busy, you know," he added, thinking of Hermione Frinton's legs.

"We can't talk here," said Vole, gazing around the room at the scattering of students and tourists.

"I told you that earlier," said Bognor with asperity.

"Man must eat. Sure you won't have a Scotch?"

"No. How long have you been here?"

Vole indicated the crossword, which was three quarter's complete. "Long enough to do that," he said.

"How many drinks have you had?"

"Not nearly enough," said Vole. "Let's eat."

Vole ordered a packet of cheese-and-onion crisps and another round of drinks. Bognor asked for a pasty. Despite his irritation with Vole, he was quite worried about him. He seemed to have disintegrated visibly since Bognor had last seen him at breakfast in College Hall. Now his clothes had a slept-in appearance. He was unshaven. And he bulged. You could not say positively that he was over-weight and yet, somehow, he bulged. Like a frog. Bognor knew the feeling. It came from overindulgence, lack of exercise and, above all, anxiety.

"I thought you'd have left Oxford by now." Bognor was being aggressively conversational. "Matter of fact, I was rather hoping I'd have to fly over to Prendergast to interview you. What kept you?"

"Research, actually." He flung a slug of whisky down his throat without appearing to swallow, and drowned it with beer. "For the book."

"Ah, the book."

"The book"—Vole prodded Bognor's chest with a fleshy forefinger—"is dynamite. I tell you, actually, it will singe not only your eyebrows, but the eyebrows of the world. *It is dynamite.*"

"What's it about, exactly?"

For some reason Vole seemed to find this question amusing. "Ha!" he exclaimed. "Ha! What's it about? Ha! What *isn't* it about, more like. I tell you what it's about. It's about LIFE."

"Oh," said Bognor, uncertain of the correct response. He hid his face and his confusion in his Guinness. When he re-emerged he tried. "What exactly about life?"

Vole gazed around the room. "Tell you later," he said loudly, "when we're outside." Then more softly he asked, "Did you like Beckenham?"

"Yes. Quite."

"You know what?" Vole was jabbing him again with that finger. Bognor had never known him so bellicosely drunk before in his life. Something had obviously happened to him in American academe. Or somewhere. "He was a shit." Vole followed this revelation with an unblinking stare, as if to indicate that he had just made a very profound and meaningful statement.

"I see," said Bognor, adding facetiously, "I suppose you've incorporated this verdict into your treatise on life."

"As a matter of fact, actually," replied Vole, jabbing away like a rejuvenated Muhammad Ali, "I have."

No more was said on the subject of Beckenham and the book until lunch was over. This lasted until closing time, which meant that Vole was even more belligerent and inebriated than before. He had almost struck Bognor for daring to suggest, albeit mildly, that cricket was, in some ways, superior, to what Vole, semi-Americanised by his years at Prendergast, persisted in calling "the ball game."

Once outside, Bognor said, "Why don't we take a turn 'round Christ Church Meadow? Unlikely to be overheard there."

Vole grunted. The day which had earlier been clear and crisp had degenerated into greyness and drizzle. Damp seemed to rise up from the ground and even out of the buildings. They walked in silence past the domed bulk of the Radcliffe Camera. Bognor recalled happy hours inside, in the library, pretending to read Gibbon and de Tocqueville while actually thinking of girls' legs and making a hundred before lunch at Lords. Leaving the Camera on their left, they cut through the alley to the left of Brasenose, crossed the High and continued towards Merton.

"Remember that dance at St. Hilda's when Scrimgeour-Harris broke his collar-bone doing the Twist?" he asked Vole.

Vole grunted again. "Scrimgeour-Harris is in Saudi, trying to sell cosmetics to the natives," he said. "I think that's what he said. May have been Kuwait, but it was certainly cosmetics."

"That was the night Badman went off with that girl of Rook's. The one with the teeth," continued Bognor.

"And bandy legs," said Vole. "She was in St. Hugh's. Reading Chemistry. I never knew what they saw in her."

"She was said to be extraordinary in bed," revealed Bognor.

"Been to bed with one," said Vole, "and you've been to bed with the lot."

Bognor considered this for a moment. They had crossed cobbled Merton Street and were passing the little memorial to the college's former pupil, Mallory, last seen with his partner Irvine, heading towards the summit of Mount Everest. That lost hero seemed light-years from this seedy present. Vole had presumably been to bed with Mrs. Vole, but Bognor doubted whether he had ever been to bed with anyone else. His remark, with which Bognor was disposed to disagree, also struck him as being ill researched. Instead of disputing it, however, Bognor said, "Your book. You were going to tell me about your book."

Vole did not reply. They passed through the iron gate into the Meadow, and walked towards the Isis. Vole scuffed at the gravel. The mist hung above the scrubby ground like steam. Bognor had never understood why the Meadow excited quite such passion. Merton Tower, squatter, but in his view more beautiful than newly renovated Magdalen, was a plus, but the Meadow was just tatty grazing land for a few scruffy cows. It had been there a long time, that was all. There were many men in Oxford who valued permanence for the sake of permanence. Bognor, personally, found change reassuring. If things stayed the same too long they unnerved him.

"How" asked Bognor, changing tack slightly, "does Beckenham come into your book?"

Vole stopped for a moment and kicked a stone with the toe of his shabby suede boot.

"Did I say that Lord Beckenham of Penge was an utter shit?"

"A shit," agreed Bognor. "Not an utter shit. Just a shit."

"Would it surprise you, Simon, to know that our late lamented Master was responsible for the deaths of many hundreds of brave and decent men?"

Bognor considered this for a moment. "Well, yes, it would, rather," he said.

"Have you ever thought," asked Vole again, "how peculiar it is that so many of the real shits went to Cambridge?"

"Not really," said Bognor. "I've always taken it for granted."

"Seriously," said Vole. "Burgess, Maclean, Philby, Blunt. All Cambridge men. And yet Oxford men are chaste as ice and pure as snow. Doesn't that strike you as odd? Particularly when you think of all the two-faced shits who were up with us. It just doesn't seem inherently plausible that Cambridge should have a monopoly of four-letter men."

"Maybe not." Bognor was doubtful.

"That's what the book's about. In part, anyway."

"About Oxford men being shits too?"

"In a manner of speaking, yes, actually." They had reached the towpath now. Even when they had been at the University there had been old college barges along this part of the river—quaint, flat-bottomed, wooden boats, ideal for parties down below and for watching the racing up above. They had gone now, replaced by spanking, modern land-based boat-houses, infinitely more practical but quite lacking in romance. One barge was still here, half-sunk and rotting. The rest had, Bognor believed, been sold to wealthy financiers, some of them in the United States. Such was progress. The old values gone, the old Masters dead, and now, it seemed, about to be discredited. Vole leaned against the railings and fished in his pocket for a cigarette. Bognor accepted one too, steeling himself for the revelation to come.

"Ever since my Mussolini book came out," said Vole, "I've been working on a study of treason."

"I thought that that Andrew Boyle, the man who exposed Blunt . . ."

Vole waved the objection aside impatiently. "Tip of the iceberg, Simon, tip of the iceberg. Mine is positively the last word. The definitive thing. No messing around. No ambiguity. Not just fourth and fifth men but whole fifth columns of them. Tens, hundreds. Dynamite. It's pure dynamite."

Bognor smiled at two pretty girls in Balliol scarves who ambled past, deep in talk. They looked impossibly young. Bognor felt his age, drew his stomach in and blew smoke out through his nose.

"Remember Cormorant, for instance," Vole was saying.

"Cormorant of All Souls'. The one who rubbished your Mussolini book?"

"Would you credit it, Simon, but he'd taken the Duce's lire. In it up to the eyeballs. An Italian spy."

Bognor whistled. "Really!" he said. "Can you prove it?"

"Naturally," said Vole. "As a matter of fact, I've got tape-recorded admissions from two of his old paymasters at the Italian Embassy and, better still, photostats of some of his reports. Piffling stuff, but totally incriminating."

"Dynamite," said Bognor, "and Beckenham was an Italian spy too? Or German? Japanese? Russian? Bolivian?"

"If you're going to be like that about it . . ." Vole chucked his cigarette away, plunged his hands into his pockets and strode off, shoulders hunched.

"Oh, God," thought Bognor, "that's done it. I've offended him." He watched the departing figure wistfully. It was rubbish, of course. Vole's mind had obviously been turned by the *TLS* review of that first book and he had founded the whole of his subsequent career on blind paranoia. Cormorant of All Souls', an Italian agent! Dear, oh dear! What next? It was even more absurd than the new lady English Fellow of Apocrypha working for British Intelligence. Or himself being a Board of Trade Special Investigator. Bognor considered this for a moment or two, glaring idiotically at his half-finished cigarette. Suddenly he threw it away. "What a life!" he murmured, as he started to trot breathlessly after his old contemporary.

"I'm sorry, I'm sorry," he panted, as he came up alongside Vole. "I didn't mean to offend you. I was being needlessly facetious. I apologise."

"It's perfectly all right," said Vole, striding on, "I'm not in the least offended. Damned silly of me to expect you to take it seriously. My mistake. Forget I even mentioned it."

"I said I was sorry," protested Bognor, surprised at Vole's turn of speed. "I just had trouble taking it seriously."

"Always was your problem," growled Vole. "Never *were* able to be serious about what mattered."

"Yes, well . . ." Bognor had to acknowledge that there was some truth in this. "Look," he said, "tell me about Beckenham. Tell me what you'd found out."

"I think, after all, I'd prefer to tell the police, if you don't mind, actually. Mitten said the Chief Inspector in charge of the case is a very decent sort and not stupid."

"True, true," agreed Bognor, remembering the way the Inspector's eyes had narrowed during question time, "but don't you think this would be better kept in the college? After all, that's the whole point of Hermione and myself being involved. We don't want the college's dirty linen being flouted about the place."

"I couldn't agree less. That's what's wrong with this country, actually, if you really want to know. Dirty linen all over the place, not being washed anywhere at all, because people are frightened the neighbours will see it. Well, this time the dirty linen is going to be run up the flag-pole for the whole world to see, as far as I'm concerned."

"Do you really think that's a good idea?"

"Frankly," said Vole, "I neither know nor care. Now that I can't thrash it out with Beckenham, I shall have to confront Aveline directly. It's not what I would have wished, but that's all there is to it. Then I shall return to Prendergast to put the finishing touches to the manuscript."

"Aveline? What's Aveline got to do with it?"

"Practically everything."

"What do you mean, practically everything?"

"Exactly what I say. But I can't expect you to understand."

They were now moving rapidly back towards the city. Bognor was afraid that once they were past the botanical gardens and into the High, Vole would do a bunk, leaving him a quarter of what, if it were true, was indeed dynamite, and arguably germane dynamite at that. It was all very peculiar and Vole seemed to him to be markedly unbalanced about it. However, Bognor's celebrated intuition was telling him to pay careful attention and allow himself no facetiousness or scepticism until much later. The idea of Aveline being some sort of traitor was as ludicrous as the idea of Cormorant being an agent of Mussolini. On the other hand . . . Bognor tried to recollect what he knew of the man. He had come to Apocrypha in the late fifties after his initial appointment as Regius Professor of Sociology. He must be all of seventy-five now, though he wore his years with a positive swagger and had a reputation, still, for cutting an enviable sexual swathe through his students of both sexes. As one of the leading sociologists in the country he had long been a significant public figure, cropping up on innumerable QUANGOS, advising credulous governments and cabinet ministers, forming popular opinion through regular articles in weekly magazines and papers. He had, in Bognor's book, been consistently bad news, though not, he had thought, as bad as Vole was now trying to make out.

"Max Aveline was recruited personally by Maisky," said Vole, "quite late in the day. Some time after nineteen forty. Maisky was Russian ambassador, remember. You think Philby's important. Philby's just an office boy compared to Aveline. He came into his own around the time of the Berlin Airlift and he was the Russians' top Brit right through till the mid-seventies. Half pay now, of course. He's a super agent emeritus."

"Never retired to Moscow?"

"Why should he?" asked Vole. "He's never been rumbled till now. He's still of use to them. Besides, he likes it here. Enjoys his creature comforts too much to live out his days in some dacha on the Caspian."

They were almost at the High Street again. Bognor was afraid he was not forgiven.

"So where does this get us apropos of Beckenham's murder?"

Vole regarded him balefully. "I should have thought even an idiot like you could see that," he said.

"No," said Bognor after a decent interval while he appeared to grope for the solution. "'Fraid not."

Vole seemed to relent a little. "Well," he said, "I must admit that at first I assumed it was suicide. Until Mitten told me about the post-mortem."

"What do you mean?"

"Simply that I had asked to have a talk with Beckenham. A proper one. And he must have realised what I wanted and that the game was up. So he must have killed himself. Or that's what I assumed."

"Wrongly, as it turned out."

"Yes."

They had arrived in the High now and were standing on the pavement near the traffic lights, at the intersection with New College Lane. The traffic was jammed as cars waited to turn. The one-way system, installed since their day, did not seem to be an unqualified success.

"So." Bognor was still at sea. "What do you think *did* happen?"

"I don't think," said Vole, "I *know*. Aveline killed him. Aveline realised I was on to Beckenham, and he thought that once I got to grips with Beckenham, the Master would talk and incriminate him. So he did him in."

"Crikey," said Bognor. "But they were muckers. Contemporaries. They'd known each other all their lives."

"Shits, too," said Vole, "like I said. They make Blunt and Philby look like a couple of girl guides."

Bognor scratched his head at the back, just where it was going baldest.

"Now," said Vole, "I must be off. I know you don't believe a word of it. I suppose I shouldn't have thought otherwise. Just thought you might have improved. Grown up a bit. But no. Ah well, never mind. One thing, though." He turned and, in a characteristically melodramatic gesture, grabbed hold of the lapels of Bognor's jacket. "Don't say anything to anyone for forty-eight hours. Not to the police. Not to Frinton. Or Mitten. Not to anyone. I need Aveline for the book. When I've got what I need, he's all yours. But first of all, he sings to me."

"I see," said Bognor. "Forty-eight hours. Tell you what. It's a deal. I won't breathe a word till the day after tomorrow. Call me at the Randolph at six p.m., day after tomorrow, and we'll see what's happened. Then, if necessary, *we*'ll have a word with Aveline."

"It's a deal," said Vole. "I'll call you at six the day after tomorrow, before I fly back to Prendergast."

"O.K." Bognor was just about to shake hands with Vole when his eye caught the passenger in a scarlet Range Rover drawn up at the traffic lights. It was Edgware. Bognor grinned and waved, but to his astonishment Edgware turned hurriedly away. Bognor looked to see if he recognised the driver. He did. It was Crutwell. At least he thought it was Crutwell. Even as he looked, the lights changed and the Range Rover drove off. "Odd," said Bognor. "That was Edgware and Crutwell in that Range Rover."

"Really," said Vole. He did not seem interested. "I should have thought Crutwell should be closeted with his spotty pupils at Ampleside. And shouldn't Edgware be at the FO?"

"He's on leave," said Bognor, "waiting for a new posting."

"I remember," said Vole. "He told me."

"They cut me dead. Most extraordinary. What do you make of that?"

"B.O.," said Vole sardonically. "Shouldn't let it worry you. I'll be in touch. Must rush. Toodle-pip."

Funny fellow, thought Bognor, as he watched Vole elbow his way through the crowds in the direction of Carfax. Was he quite sane? Even if he were paranoid and unhinged, was there enough in his theory to suggest a real verdict? Should he say anything to Smith or to Hermione, or should he keep his promise? Could Aveline have done it? That was the key question. If it was the Master's glass that had been doctored, then it had to have been done by someone drinking in Mitten's rooms that evening. But if the bottle had been diluted, could it have been someone else? Except that anyone else would have had to have got into Mitten's dining room (not in itself too difficult) and then into Mitten's drink cupboard (difficult or not? Impossible to say as yet. Must find out if Mitten kept it locked) .

As these questions were racketing around Bognor's mind, he was walking up the High in Vole's footsteps. It was late afternoon now and he had a choice. At Carfax, the Piccadilly Circus or Times Square of Oxford, he could turn right or left. Right would take him to the Randolph and thence on to Hermione Frinton, a large gin and tonic and who knows what. That way led temptation. It was attractive but it was not what he really ought to do. If he turned left and walked down St. Aldate's and past Christ Church, he would come to Apocrypha, that elegant, opulent pile so

Pembrdul ?

envied by "The House," its larger but less stylish and successful neighbour. That way lay the Inspector's incident
room. That way lay duty. He knew what he ought to do,
yet still he faltered. Then a newspaper hoarding caught his
eye: "DEAD MASTER SHOCK."

Nervously he bought an Oxford *Mail* and scanned the
lead story. It was headed: "Lord Beckenham. It was
Murder!" The story was straightforward enough. It clearly
emanated, as Bognor had feared it would, from the office of
the city coroner. There were quotes from Chief Inspector
Smith and from Mitten, but these were so anodyne as to
be meaningless. It hardly mattered. The news was out.
From now on they had the press to contend with. Bognor
had some experience of the press and, knowing what he
did, he was depressed.

To proceed straight to Hermione Frinton's flat was now
out of the question. With heavy heart and even heavier
legs (quite sore, too, since he had been walking for at least
an hour and a half now and was not used to it) he set off
for Apocrypha.

As he turned left through the tiny door set in the great
gates (presented by Charles II to replace those looted by a
mob of Diggers and Levellers during the Protectorate), he
collided with a female figure on her way out. For a moment there was some mutual confusion, but in a gentle-
manly manner he retreated almost at once, and stood aside
to let the lady pass. She was about to do this when she suddenly stopped dead in her tracks and exclaimed: "*Gott in
Himmel!* It's Simon Bognor of the Board of Trade!"

"Yes," he said nervously, recognising the voice but unable to put a name to it. The woman was wearing a suede
jacket with the collar turned very high, a costermonger's
cap pulled down over the face, and a pair of the most enormous sun-glasses he had ever seen. Consequently there was
not much to recognise. The scent, musky and expensive,
was as familiar as the voice, but that might, he thought, be

because it was the same as Hermione Frinton had been wearing this morning.

"*How* marvellous!" The woman kissed him noisily on both cheeks. She'd been drinking. Gin. Probably not since lunch, but the smell triggered his memory.

It was Molly Mortimer of the *Daily Globe*. He was very fond of Molly. He had, briefly, shared an office with her during the unfortunate business of the St. John Derby murder. They had not met since. Monica disapproved of their relationship and though nothing had, quite, come of it, her instinct, like her husband's, was, as usual, sound. Normally he would have been overjoyed to see her. Any time but now, for he had a strong suspicion that she was going to be a nuisance.

"Hello," said Bognor, staggering slightly under the impact of the embrace. Molly, like nearly all the women he ran into, was bigger than him. "Fancy seeing you here." He realised forlornly that these words were delivered in an unflatteringly sepulchral voice.

"Oh all right, be like that," said Molly, mock grumpily. "Are you here for the opposition? Don't tell me you've taken up journalism for real. What *are* you doing here?"

"I happened to be passing," said Bognor. "Pure coincidence. And I thought I'd drop in on my old tutor."

"I'd forgotten you were an Apocrypha man. I thought you were in Balliol."

"No," said Bognor. "I may have said that, but it was part of the disguise. Like saying I worked on the Winnipeg *Eagle*."

"Well, well," Molly exclaimed, "*que suerte!* What about a drinkie?"

"Um," said Bognor, "er, I actually think I'd better nip in and see if he's in. But I could always join you for a jar a little later." He thought glumly of his receding appointment with Hermione. Life was not treating him entirely fairly. "Anyway, what are you doing here?"

"Covering this murder lark," said Molly. "They took me off the Pepys Column and put me in the news-room. This is *exactly* my sort of story. Lots of scope for colour. Dons are such dears and it's such *bloody* good fun sending them up. They pretend to complain, but they love it, really. Don't you think?"

"Well," said Bognor.

"Oh, Simon," she exclaimed petulantly, "don't be such an old grouch. What are you really doing here? I'll bet you're up to something. Are you staying in town?"

"At the Randolph."

"Aha!" Molly was triumphant. "In that case you're unquestionably up to something. You wouldn't be staying if you weren't. Let's have dinner."

"I, er . . ." said Bognor.

"Fine. That's settled then. I'll see you in the bar at the Randolph at seven-thirty."

"Right," said Bognor, "seven-thirty it is." He tried to sound enthusiastic. It was not that he didn't like Molly, just that he would have preferred . . . "Oh, bloody hell!" he exclaimed as he hurried through the lodge and on towards the Shakespeare Room. It was all becoming too much. Too many people were clamouring for his attention. Temptations were everywhere, and back home in London he was being observed. Monica was waiting to chastise him for any suspicion of infidelity, real or imagined; for any excess to do with food, drink or women. Meanwhile Parkinson, ever eager to admonish him for those derelictions of duty to which he was unfortunately prone, had now been reinforced by the insufferable Lingard, the oily little twerp sent by Teddington to spy on him. His every step was being watched and he hated it. Even here, out in the field, he was under constant surveillance by Mitten and by Hermione Frinton and Chief Inspector Chappie, and now Molly, who was far too keen a journalist to respect a confidence. It meant that he would have to watch his drinking at dinner. In his present mood, he decided, he would like nothing more than to go to bed, alone, save for a good book, a hot-water bottle and a whisky toddy.

Instead, he was bound for the incident room, alias the Shakespeare Room, where twenty years ago he had sung madrigals and rounds with the Apocrypha Glee Club, listened to interminable learned papers at the Lecky (Historical) Society and the Trollope (English Literature) Club (founded after another distinguished Apocrypha man). In lighter and more drunken vein, there had been a frivolous debating society called the Arkwright and Blennerhasset (named after two of the college's most generous benefactors). This too had met in the Shakespeare Room, which was large enough to accommodate about a hundred people. It was on the ground floor, with French windows leading onto a new terrace (presented by a distinguished, now-assassinated African alumnus), which in turn led onto lawns which fell away towards the river by Folly Bridge. Bognor had played croquet on this lawn throughout his final summer. It had not helped with his final exams.

"Come." The Inspector's voice was out of character. It did not sit well with his memories. Nor did the Shakespeare Room which was now equipped with telephones, maps, charts and two policewomen.

"Hello, there," said the Inspector, who was sitting in his shirt-sleeves, surrounded by paper. "You'll have seen the evening paper?"

Bognor nodded. "Rather a bore," he said. "Inevitable, I suppose."

"I suppose so, yes. Some of the press are here already. Woman from the *Daily Globe* came barging in here only a few minutes ago. Don't know how she got here so quickly. Not a bad looker."

"No," agreed Bognor. "I passed her on my way in."

"Ho. Know her, do you?" The Inspector looked conspiratorial. Bognor did not care for the expression and its implications. He suspected Monica was correct in her accusations. Chief Inspector Smith was the sort of man who was heavily into dirty magazines. It was on the tip of Bognor's tongue to ask if he had ever worked on the vice squad. But he did not.

"We worked together, briefly, a few years ago. The St. John Derby murder. You may remember."

"When Lord Wharfedale and his son . . . ? Remember it. I should think I do. Went from bad to worse. Hope we're not going to have anything like that here. One murder at a time is an ample sufficiency."

"I couldn't agree more," said Bognor, "but if you're dealing with a homicidal maniac you can never be too sure."

The Inspector looked quizzically at his colleague from the Board of Trade. "Think this is a Master-killer do you? Maybe we should put a twenty-four-hour guard on the heads of all Oxford colleges? Maybe we're dealing with a candidate for admission who got turned down. Or someone with a grudge against authority."

"Sorry," said Bognor, puzzled, "I didn't mean to seem frivolous. For once."

"No? Well. That's all right. Long day." The Inspector sighed. "And we're nowhere near a solution. Haven't even got the washing-up back from the labs. How was Vole?"

"Oh," said Bognor, "no help I'm afraid. He just wanted to talk about his research project." That was true as far as it went, he thought. He did not greatly care for Vole, but a confidence was a confidence and he was certainly not going to betray it to a dirty-minded policeman. In the forty-eight hours he would tell the Chappie. Not before.

"What's he like, Vole?" asked the Inspector. "Any grounds for suspecting him?"

"Not that I'm aware of. He's an assistant professor at a small but smart university in the United States. Clever, able, reasonably successful. No visible axe to grind with the Master, nor anyone else, come to that."

"Hmmm." The policeman leaned back in his chair and

pushed the end of a pencil into his mouth, rattling his teeth with it. Then he removed it, tilted the chair back to an upright position, and wrote on a piece of foolscap. "Mind if we just run through the characters of our main suspects?" he asked. "I'll be seeing them in person, but it would help to have some leads."

"All right. But I can't be a lot of help. The Gaudy was the first time I'd seen most of them for twenty years."

"Understood," said Smith, "though twenty years ago may be exactly what we need. I have the impression our motives for this crime are embedded in the past. That's when you and your friends knew Beckenham best. Take you, for instance. Don't suppose you'd seen the old boy much since you left?"

"No," agreed Bognor. "He'd hardly crossed my mind, let alone my threshold."

"No correspondence? No phone conversations about the good old days? No teatime reminiscences at his London club?"

"We didn't have that sort of relationship. And I wasn't exactly a favoured son."

"Not *un*-favoured?" Smith screwed his eyes up in his suspicious expression.

"No, not at all. Just a bit, well"—Bognor flushed— "run of the mill. Apocrypha was—is—a rather special place. Unless you were going to get a first, or edit *Isis*, or be President of the Union or win at least one blue, no one paid any real attention to you. Excellence was the only thing which *really* rated. Super-excellence. I was pretty solid beta with occasional spectacular descents to gamma."

"And the others? Edgware, Vole, Rook and Crutwell?"

Bognor smiled wistfully. "Golden boys," he said, "all of them in their different ways. Firsts, each one of them, though how Humphrey Rook did it I'll never know. He wasn't as clever as the others, and he was bone idle. It was his political theory that turned the scales, apparently. Pure alpha. Purest alpha anyone had seen in years. Couldn't understand it myself. We did political theory tutes together and I thought his essays were the most turgid imaginable. The Master thought so too, as far as I can remember."

"And you did not get a pure alpha, I suppose." Smith grinned condescendingly.

"Beta query gamma," said Bognor. "Story of my life."

Smith's smile seemed more sympathetic this time.

"Tell me about Rook," he said.

Bognor sighed involuntarily and thought back to his first encounter with Rook. It had been at the Apocrypha scholarship exam. They had been billeted together on the same staircase. He remembered how precocious Rook had seemed, infinitely more adult than any of the other candidates. He had kept a bottle of Dubonnet in his room and smoked Abdulla Turkish cigarettes. Also, he had been seen with a woman, or, to be more accurate, a girl from Cranborne Chase. The girl wore fish-net stockings and great streaks of eye-shadow, both of which rendered her even more inaccessible and intimidating to Bognor and his equally callow fellow candidates. It had been the same when they came up at the beginning of their first term. Rook began by wearing a smoking jacket and affecting to be a disciple of, first, Bakunin and later Kropotkin. Bognor now doubted whether he had actually read either, but at the time he, having barely heard of either of the two Russian anarchists, was suitably impressed. It was noticeable that Rook was a creature of fad. He switched unceasingly from one guru to another so that it was virtually impossible for anyone to keep either pace or track. Such was indeed his intention.

"He'd got himself very well organised," said Bognor. "He decided to cut a figure and he did it. His main aim in life was upstaging the rest of us. I think he knew he didn't have the intellect to take the Voles and Crutwells on at their own game. So he dictated the terms himself."

"And it worked?"

"Yes," said Bognor, "I think it did."

"No discernible motive, though?"

"None that I can see."

"And now"—Smith was ruminative—"has he fulfilled that youthful promise? Is he still a poseur and a con-man?"

"He's something in the city."

"Does that answer my question?" Smith seemed uncertain.

"I think so. He's joined the Church of England and the Tory Party."

Smith raised his eyebrows. "Bit out of character, isn't it?"

"Not really. He's always been a step or two ahead of the game. He joined the Conservatives just before it became acceptable again, and he hit the religious bandwagon in the same way. I agree Roman Catholicism would have been smarter, but I think there's a will he's afraid of getting cut out of."

"Does he have a seat, or a prospective one?"

"The buzz is," said Bognor, "that he's the front runner for Sheen Central, which is about as safe as Cheltenham."

Smith made a neat note. "That's Rook and Vole," he said. "What about Edgware and Crutwell?"

"Heavenly twins," said Bognor, none too kindly. "Permanent haloes. Scarcely separable, either. They did everything together. They were joint Presidents of the Arkwright and Blennerhasset; they played Algernon and Ernest in the College production of *The Importance*, they shared the Newdigate poetry prize and in their final year they lived together in digs in Holywell."

"Lived together?" Smith arched his eyebrows.

"Not in that way." Bognor scratched his scalp absentmindedly, "At least, I don't think so, although now that you mention it, there was something *spooky* about their relationship."

"Did they have women?"

Bognor thought. He had been rather incurious about

other people's sexual relationships. On the whole, he was inclined to think that most of the sex was being carried on by a small minority. He, of course, had had Monica most of the time. Crutwell and Edgware had always been surrounded by women. Men too. Safety in numbers? Innocence, perhaps.

"I honestly don't know," he said. "I'd be quite surprised if they had anyone in particular. They dispensed charm evenly. No fear. No favour."

"Promiscuous, you mean?" said Smith, a little too eagerly.

"No. I don't think so. I think they were too busy being elegant and witty and wonderful to have much time for sex."

"Homosexual?"

"It honestly hadn't occurred to me before," said Bognor, "but now that you mention it, well, yes, I suppose it is just possible. Crutwell used to be quite pretty. Still is. Edgware was more macho. And I think they shared a study at whatever school they were at. Stowe, I think. Or Uppingham. Somewhere up there."

"They didn't consort with known homosexuals?"

"There weren't many *known* homosexuals," said Bognor, a shade peevishly. "One or two dons. A dreadful pouf in Magdalen who used to dress exclusively in lime green."

"Not a profitable line of enquiry, then?"

"Not particularly."

Smith scratched at his notes. "And what happened to *them?* They presumably became separable at last?"

"Both married, with children. Ultra-conventional and respectable. Edgware is a great whizz in the FO. Just back from Moscow, a year or so on the Soviet desk and then who knows what? A key job, that's certain."

"And Crutwell?"

Bognor told him about Crutwell's job at Ampleside and about his aspirations at Sherborne, Cranlingham and

Fraffleigh. Smith scribbled and smiled. At last he seemed satisfied.

"Good," he said. "Now we're getting somewhere."

"Oh?" Bognor could not see that they were getting anywhere at all, but he was certainly not going to admit it to Chief Inspector Chappie. "I must be getting back," he said. "I'm meeting someone."

"Not the delectable Dr. Frinton, by any chance?" asked the policeman, smiling greasily.

"No," said Bognor, wishing it was.

"Ah." Smith rubbed his hands. "Will Mrs. Bognor be joining you in Oxford?"

"Depends how long I'm here for," he said. "She'll come at the weekend unless we're finished by then."

"You must bring her out to meet the missus," said the Inspector, "sample the dandelion and burdock. Amazing what you can do with these homemade wine kits. The Moselle-style elderberry takes your breath away, and as for the blackberry claret . . ."

"Sounds wonderful." Bognor fingered his collar. He could just imagine Monica's expression when she learned that she was going to a wine tasting given by the would-be rapist of her youth. "Meanwhile, though, what are we going to do about the press?" he asked gingerly.

"As little as possible. Main thing is to stop your friend Mitten talking to them. I have the impression he quite fancies having his name and picture all over the papers."

"Won't do him any good if he's really after the Mastership," said Bognor. "The one thing the Apocrypha High Table values is discretion. The only time any of them talk to the press is when they win a Nobel Prize. And that only happens every other year."

Bognor got up to go. Suddenly he felt exhausted. It had been a gruelling day. He felt very tired. Quite apart from the intellectual effort involved in a day of heavy sleuthing, he was physically exhausted, too. He hadn't walked so far in years. His suedes were not made for it, nor, he reflected, wincing, were his feet, which had grown flat with age and neglect. He wasn't at all sure he hadn't got an ingrowing toenail. And a blister. If he had been at home Monica would have made him a mustard bath. As it was, he had an ordeal by Molly Mortimer to endure. And he was still rather hoping he might be able to take in the promised gin and tonic *chez* Frinton.

It was chilly in the street. He turned up his collar and began to mooch lugubriously north towards the Randolph. Who would have thought, in those days of their gilded youth, *their* gilded youth, not his, that they would have ended up as murder suspects. And the Master's murderers at that. What had they got in common, he asked himself as he tracked along the wall of Christ Church, past Trevor-Roper's old house. MA Oxon, the shared experience of three years in the superior splendour of Apocrypha, but was there anything else? The others still saw the world from a vantage point of success, but for himself very little had gone right since he left the university. Getting a place at Apocrypha was, one might say, his last real achievement. What had he got to look forward to but more footling years investigating piffling misdeeds and infringements of the regulations on behalf of the perfectly bloody Board of Trade. Unless his request for transfer actually came through. Perhaps he would be posted to the FO. Who knows, he might find himself sent as third secretary to Ulan Bator. With Edgware as Ambassador. That would be a turn up for the book. Not that they would send a young Turk like Edgware to anywhere as God-forsaken as Mongolia. Not even as his country's youngest Ambassador.

He paused at the traffic lights. Funny, that. He and Edgware both at a turning point in their lives. Edgware waiting for his significant next job, the one that would mark him out as a high flier who was coming good, a bright white hope sustained. Himself hanging in desperately for a release from the quagmire of the Board of Trade. Very different rites of passage, yet both turning points. At least they had that in common, he and Edgware. Youth now irrevocably behind them, they waited for the first assignment of middle years. He frowned. Was that a clue? He crossed the street and shuffled on rapt in thought, muttering. Crutwell too. He was at a moment of choice, decision —destiny, even. Headmastership loomed. He would get one. Naturally. But if he didn't, he would end his life as Mr. Chips. Yes, that was the choice: Mr. Chips or Dr. Arnold.

Edgware, himself, Crutwell. What about Vole? Vole's book was a vital part of his life. It had not only obsessed him for years, it was a necessary passport to the next rung on the ladder. A professional success would mean a full professorship, invitations to lecture, to contribute learned papers to learned journals. A failure would consign him permanently to the academic dustbin. "Vole?" they would mutter in Senior Common Rooms whenever his name came up for an Oxford fellowship, "wasn't he the man who wrote that rather dim book on traitors and fellow travellers?" And on receiving the answer "yes" they would sniff into their port and pass on to the next candidate.

Bognor was at the Randolph. He walked into the foyer with a new lightness of step. A theory was emerging. A half-baked theory to be sure, in fact so flimsy a theory that it could hardly be dignified with the name. It was hardly ready for baking at all, and yet it was a beginning of sorts. There was Rook, too—front runner for Sheen Central. And Mitten, perhaps he really did covet the mastership. Quite what all this had to do with the murder he couldn't say. But suddenly he found that he was almost looking forward to dinner.

There were two messages waiting in reception. One from Monica and one from Hermione Frinton. Neither contained anything except a request to telephone, but the porter who handed him the notes, together with the room keys, favoured him with a knowing look which Bognor did not enjoy. He did not return it but merely accepted what was his and went upstairs to bath. He frowned and whistled in the lift, mild elation and definite perplexity storming about in his brain like a cerebral Punch and Judy. It was like getting the first word in a three-part crossword clue. Practically all the suspects had careers in the balance, but so what? Why should Peter Crutwell murder the Master because he wanted to be Headmaster of Fraffleigh? Or Ian Edgware because he wanted a key job in Washington or Brussels and not a back number in Bogotá?

He turned on the bath and emptied a few drops of Balenciaga bath oil (souvenir of an earlier misadventure) into the tub, then went to phone Monica. She would be able to throw a little light. She was good at that. Regular little spotlight. One thing, though, there was no way Vole could have done it. Not if Beckenham was the missing link in his masterpiece. He'd hardly have done the old boy in just as he was on the point of coughing up. Unless, of course, Vole had founded his theories on a complete mistake. If so, then Beckenham would have sent the whole edifice crumbling like the proverbial pack of cards. Vole's book would have vanished. So maybe that's it, he thought gingerly. Vole realised that the Master was the missing spoke rather than the missing link and so he murdered him. Once he was safely dead he could vilify him to his heart's content. Common practice these days to speak ill of the dead. In fact, the dead seemed to him to be getting an increasingly raw deal in this barbaric age. No one had a good word to say for them.

"Monica?" His wife's voice interrupted his ramblings.

"Yes."

"Me."

"So I hear."

"Yes. Well. You O.K.?"

"Fine, thank you very much. And you?"

Bognor wondered why she was being so polite. Sloping

off for a Rhogan Jhosht with some old lover as soon as his back was turned, he shouldn't wonder. Guilt. That was it.

"I need some help," he said.

"Surprise me."

"Don't be unpleasant. You were being so nice a moment or two."

She laughed. Not unpleasantly, but with the relaxed condescension of a woman who has lived with a man for years and knows his faults. As a matter of fact, Monica preferred Bognor's faults to his virtues, and she enjoyed being leaned on.

"I'm not being unpleasant," she said. "I just know what's coming. You've got some bits of jigsaw but you can't fit them together."

"Something like that," conceded Bognor. "I don't want to say too much on the phone." He lowered his voice. "There are one or two of the staff here I'm not too keen on. The point is that all our suspects were at a crossroads."

"Crossroads?"

"Metaphorically speaking, if you follow. They were all in for jobs, promotions, advancements, things like that."

"And you think that may make a motive?"

"It had crossed my mind."

"Darling, I hate to remind you but I've already suggested that motive, only you don't want them *all* to have motives." She sighed. "I mean, you're not going to make out that they all did it. Like *Murder on the Orient Express.*"

"No," said Bognor unhappily, "I suppose not. Only it did seem a funny coincidence."

"Not that I can see," said Monica briskly. "You're all, what, in your late thirties to early forties? That's a very significant stage in a man's life. It would be surprising if you *weren't* all set for change."

"I suppose so." Bognor felt let down. "I thought I was getting somewhere," he ventured.

"Well." She paused to take a drink of something. Bog-

nor heard her swallowing. Next door, the bath water was
still running. "All I can see is references. But if they were
all little heroes why should that worry them? You have to
find skeletons in their cupboards."

Bognor thought about this. Before long his bath water
would start to overflow. And he still had to call Hermione.
Besides which, he didn't have long in which to change for
Molly. Suddenly life seemed fraught with complication.

"Are you saying that they'd have named the Master as a
reference?"

"Seems likely."

Bognor rubbed his paunch absent-mindedly and contemplated his youth as if down a reversed telescope.

"But it's such a long time ago."

"What's twenty years in a man approaching meno-
pause?"

"But an evening gone," admitted Bognor, "nevertheless . . ."

"Don't you 'nevertheless' me, Simon Bognor," said
Monica sharply. "Who better to cite in one's defence than
the Master of Apocrypha?"

"And who more damaging to have as a witness for the
prosecution?" Bognor spoke ruefully. "I must go," he said,
and he put the phone down hurriedly, wishing his wife a
quite perfunctory good night.

Then, until he heard ominous sounds from the bathroom he sat on the bed picking abstractedly at his toe-
nails. Something was not quite right, but he still couldn't
put his finger on it. Nor did the bath, disgracefully over-
full, help him much. Normally he found hot water condu-
cive to incisive thought. But not tonight.

He lay back and watched his toes, a line of amphibious
pink piglets, as they traced patterns in the soapy water.
"Which little pig dunnit?" he murmured to himself. Then
raising his voice he said, "Let us suppose that Piglet A is
on the short list for a vital new appointment. Let us sup-

pose that his potential employers approach the Master of Apocrypha for a reference. Let us further suppose that the Master is disposed to give a good reference. Then Piglet A has no motive for murdering the Master. QED. Let us, however, suppose that the Master is inclined to give our little piglet an absolute stinker of a reference, thus effectively screwing up his chances of advancement. That's a murder motive, all right. Let us suppose on the other trotter, as it were, that the Master of Apocrypha *is* going to give Piglet A an award-winning reference and that this is known to Piglet B, who is an enemy of Piglet A and therefore wishes to do him down. In this case the murderer would turn out to be Piglet B." He sighed and hooked the plug chain round the big toe of his right foot and yanked it out with a flourish. If he was on the right track, then Chief Inspector Chappie was right about twenty years ago being the place to look. No use delving about in the present. He climbed out, wrapped a towel round his middle and padded into the bedroom, dripping.

"I am terribly sorry," he said when Hermione answered. "It's been one of those days."

"Your gin's still in the fridge," she said. "Are you going to be able to collect?"

"I don't know," said Bognor, "I'm still hoping. But I'm afraid someone's cropped up unexpectedly."

"Aha."

"But perhaps we could do it after dinner."

"Do *what* after dinner?" Dr. Frinton managed to sound both shocked and suggestive.

"Have that drink," said Bognor, "and a talk. There are one or two things I want to discuss."

"Like what?" She sounded a little put out by the prosaic quality of his responses.

"Well," he began, "I've got an idea. Or the beginnings of an idea."

She said nothing.

"The thing is," he tried again, "I just wondered if you knew whether or not any of our suspects asked old Beckenham for a reference recently."

"I don't, but it's easily discovered."

"Oh?"

"Even the Masters of Oxford colleges have filing systems," she said, "so it won't be difficult to find out."

"Oh." Bognor frowned again. He seemed to remember that the question of "files" had been crucial in the revolting later sixties. On one occasion a group of student stormtroopers had invaded the dean's rooms and demanded to have his "files" in order that they could be burned. The dean had denied the existence of files but admitted, with a suitably menacing smile of triumph, that he had an exceedingly efficient memory which he would not hesitate to use when necessary. Bognor could not remember whether that had been Ashburner, the rather unsatisfactory Dean of Apocrypha, or Willis-Bund, his more impressive counterpart at Balliol. He rather fancied it was Willis-Bund. Ashburner did not have a memory worthy of the name.

"Would that sort of thing be filed then?" he asked.

"Natch," said Hermione. "Beckenham had everyone filed by year. Very efficient."

"You've seen them then?"

"Not to read. Nobody read them except Beckenham. But I made it my business to know where they were and how they were organised. I'll go and dig them out now if you like. We can discuss them after dinner if you can't think of anything more stimulating."

"You won't be able to take them away," said Bognor.

"Don't you believe it." Her voice suggested, with some conviction, that she could do exactly what she liked, when and where she liked and how she liked.

"Wouldn't look good though. Our chief inspector friend wouldn't be pleased. Nor Mitten. I'll come with you. We'll look at them in situ."

"After dinner?"

"After dinner," he agreed. "I'll call when I'm through."

"I'll pick you up," she said. "I have wheels."

"Right." Bognor replaced the receiver and dried very carefully between his toes. He had an unreasonable terror of athlete's foot. Then he dressed slowly and methodically. In a spirit of wistful nostalgia he had packed an Arkwright and Blennerhasset tie. He seldom wore it, if only because pink and purple stripes drew attention to his worsening complexion, but tonight, he decided, was exceptional. It was, quite apart from anything else, the sort of tie Molly Mortimer would enjoy.

CHAPTER 4

He was right about that. The first thing she said as he
walked into the bar where she was stirring the olive round
her dry martini with a gloomy concentration was: "I say,
that's an Arkwright and Blennerhasset."

"Yes," he agreed. "How did you know?"

Molly scrutinised the olive yet more closely and then
put it in her mouth and grimaced. "One, because in this
job you have to be good at ties. I can tell a Grid from an
Ampleforth at forty paces. There's not much you can't
deduce from a man's neckwear. And two, because my
Cousin Humphrey was an A and B member. Not that he's
worn his for bloody ages, but he used to. Once seen, never
forgotten. What's your poison?"

Bognor said he'd like a Scotch.

"Cousin?"

"Yes." She raised her glass to him. "Chin-chin," she
said. "Long-time. You look well."

Bognor grinned ruefully. He did not look well. Never
did. She didn't look particularly well either, which was not
really surprising since she lived most of her life indoors
and in semi-darkness. She also smoked and drank. Nevertheless, she had undeniable glamour. It was certainly not
the glamour of first youth, and it had to be admitted that
she looked her age and more. Fortyish, he supposed. What
made her so alluring was the sense of harmless corruption
about her. You felt she must have tried everything once.

"A cousin called Humphrey in the Arkwright and
Blennerhasset? Not Humphrey Rook by any chance?"

"The same." She smiled. "He said he knew you. In fact,

he said he'd seen you the other night at the Apocrypha
Gaudy."

"Goodness. I never knew."

"No reason why you should."

"I suppose not." He sipped and pondered. "Where shall
we eat?" he asked.

"I booked a table at a new Italian place round the
corner. I hope that's all right. The *Globe* will pay."

"And how will you justify that?"

She shrugged disdainfully. "You know perfectly well
that the only justifying we have to do is profoundly perfunctory. I shall put down 'Dinner with contact from
Board of Trade.'"

"And they'll wear that?"

"I should bloody well hope so. I'm here to do a piece
about the Master's murder. They're hardly going to quib-
ble over my entertaining the chap in charge of the case."

"I'm not in charge of the case."

"So you said." She raised her glass and gazed at him
knowingly from under fluttering and very false eyelashes.

"Is Gringe still running the Diary?" he asked, in an obvious attempt to deflect her questioning, which she acknowledged by looking still more knowing than before.
She obviously decided to accept his decision, however, so
that until they had gone round the corner and eaten half-
way through a quite passable Italian meal they gossiped
about old times and old friends.

Eventually she said, "And how did Cousin Humphrey
seem at your Gaudy?"

"Oh, you know Humphrey," said Bognor, swallowing the
last of his *saltimbocca*. "*Comme ci, comme ça.*"

Molly digested this remark together with her *bocconcini*
and said, "I wouldn't describe Humphrey as being in the
least bit *comme ci, comme ça.*"

"And how would you describe him?"

"Absolutely ruthless and single-minded and prepared to
resort to anything to achieve his ambitions." She pushed

her plate away and took a cigarette from her bag. "Including murder."

"He never struck me as being like that."

"Liar."

"White liar, maybe. I admit he has always seemed a little bit unscrupulous."

"*Little* bit. Ha! That's a laugh. I mean it. He'd do anything. Anything at all, if it was for the good of Humphrey Rook."

"But he's a born-again Christian. Or something."

"Well, there you are then." She blew smoke down her nose with a little bray of triumph. "You don't think he believes it? He just thinks it goes down well at Tory Party selection meetings. And how right he is. He'd do anything."

"Do you mean that? Anything? Literally?"

She appeared to consider this for a moment, eyes creased in concentration. "Yes," she said at last, "literally."

"You're not"—Bognor toyed with his glass—"trying to imply anything?"

"Like what?" she enquired.

"Like that he murdered the Master."

"Naughty, naughty," said Molly. "You're not supposed to be here on business. You're just passing through. Remember?"

"Yes." Bognor flushed and ordered coffee and a couple of cognacs from a passing waiter. "Well," he continued, "that's perfectly correct, but one does have one's professional curiosity. And now that it transpires that poor Lord Beckenham didn't have a heart attack but was done to death by person or persons unknown . . . Well, as I say, one does have one's professional curiosity."

"I suppose one does." Molly smiled. "Would your professional curiosity extend to wanting to hear that Cousin Humphrey had a motive? No"—she shook her head—"I don't suppose it would. Not as you're just passing through. Oh well, just a thought."

Bognor sulked. He knew she knew. She knew he knew she knew. And so on. Impasse. Boring.

"Tell you what." Molly held her brandy balloon in the palm of her hand and swilled it around slowly, smiling. Her face was lined and the candle was so ineptly positioned that it managed to accentuate the grooves in her skin, picking out the crow's-feet and the laugh lines when it should, if the restaurateur had known his business better, have softened them. Taken some years off. Bognor didn't mind. He preferred her like that. He liked mutton to be dressed as mutton—dressed to kill, perhaps, but never dressed as lamb.

"What?" he asked, quite gently.

"I'll trade you," she replied, "make you a swap."

"I don't have anything you'd be interested in."

"Don't kid yourself." She fluttered the false eyelashes again. Not without reason. There had been moments in the past. Or almost. I'll give you Cousin Humphrey's motive. And in return you admit that you're here on business and promise me an exclusive as soon as you know who done the dirty deed."

"Um." Bognor chewed on his brandy. It seemed to him that merely by agreeing to this rather absurd swap he was admitting his interest. But suppose her information was good. A motive for Rook? That would be useful.

"Don't you like your cousin?"

"Not in the least, since you ask. But that's not what I'm asking. Do you agree? Is it a deal?"

"Um," Bognor repeated, and then with a singularly unconvincing display of indifference, "If you like."

"I do," she said.

"O.K." He smiled. "Go ahead. Surprise me."

"You remember that Humphrey got a first?"

"Of course. It's not the sort of thing he'd let you forget, even if you wanted to."

"And you must admit it was surprising."

"Certainly. He and I were natural thirds."

"So what was your theory?"

"Human error," said Bognor. "Happens all the time. The Oxford class system's notorious for it. All the first-class men get thirds. Well, not all, but an awful lot. Half the examiners are jealous. That's got a lot to do with it. They got brilliant un-viva'd firsts hundreds of years ago in the dim and distant, and here they are exactly where they've always been, marking the very same exam papers that got them here in the first place. They are chronically embittered."

"Sounds like special pleading." Molly fingered one of her gaudy drop earrings.

"Not really." Bognor spoke without regret. "I was a natural third, just like Edgware and Crutwell and Vole were natural firsts. For what that's worth. I'm not sure it has much to do with the great battle of life. I'm not convinced it has any real importance at all, though it seemed to at the time. Especially for Rook."

"Yes, Cousin Humphrey was always very anxious to succeed."

"Do tell," said Bognor, mock impatiently. "The suspense is killing."

"You may or may not know," she said, "that Humphrey's first was based mainly on one paper."

"Political theory. I was talking about it just now to Chief Inspector . . . er . . . that is I . . ." He blushed crimson. "Oh," he said, "blown it."

She smiled triumphantly, but nevertheless with kindness. "You are a funny little man," she said, "a very funny little man. And there are times when I could eat you up." She gazed at him fondly as if he were some peculiarly appealing pudding.

"Does this mean you aren't going to tell me Cousin Humphrey's motive?" he asked, cross with himself, maddened at committing such a ridiculous gaffe.

She considered. "No, no," she announced at last, "I think it would be unfair to tantalise. Besides, I'm not one to withhold evidence from the police. Even when the police come in such a bizarre form as yourself."

Bognor did not comment.

"Cousin Humphrey was taught political theory by the Master?"

"Correct. We did it together. The old boy spent most of his time banging on about his impressions of Attlee and what it was like being in Harold Wilson's cabinet. He knew practically nothing about political theory but he was quite good on political practice. So you'd take in an essay on Hobbes or Hegel and end up talking about the nationalisation of the railways or the partition of India."

"And the Master liked Humphrey?"

This Bognor was forced to concede. He had, in fact, liked Humphrey Rook very much indeed, had even been in some awe of him. It was something to do with the attraction of opposites. The Master, devious though he could be, was, in essence, a high-grade plodder. Rook was a terrible chancer. There was no way in which the Master could or would have played fast and loose with the cards life had dealt him in the way that Rook did. In a way he was appalled but in another he was mesmerised. He also had the self-made man's exaggerated respect for what he considered the natural or aristocratic advantages of others. And Rook had been to school at Harrow.

Bognor nodded. "Lord Beckenham was very keen on your Cousin Humphrey."

"So if I were to tell you that he covered up for him you wouldn't be altogether surprised."

"Covered up? How do you mean?"

"À la Watergate. A Nixon style cover-up."

"You've lost me." Bognor wondered whether he should order more brandy. He was about to become confused. "You mean that Humphrey Rook was working for the Master in some undercover operation, got found out and was bailed out by the old boy himself?

"No. He wasn't working *for* the Master. The Master

caught him red-handed and didn't let on. Except that he did tell Uncle Bert."

"Uncle Bert?"

"Humphrey's father. My uncle Bert. He's Chairman of Chippenhams."

"Hang on." Bognor now called for two more brandies and concentrated hard. "The Master caught him red-handed, but doing what? With a woman, do you mean?"

"More likely to be a boy. Women aren't exactly Humphrey's style. Or hadn't you noticed?"

"Not really."

"No." Molly Mortimer laughed with a smoky purring noise from the back of the throat. "Not many do. Anyway, this had nothing to do with sex. Evidently, one day Humphrey went to see the Master on some pretext or other; only the Master wasn't there. The door of his study was open, though, so Humphrey went in and, being Humphrey, had a bit of a snoop at the papers on his desk."

The second brandies arrived. Molly paused, extracting the maximum possible theatricality from the moment.

"As you may recall," she continued, as the waiter departed, "Lord Beckenham was responsible for setting the political theory paper that year. And when Humphrey started poking around almost the first thing he saw was the proof copy, and whereas you or I might have had a quick gander and then made a swift and discreet withdrawal, Cousin Humphrey sat down and started copying the questions out."

"Taking a bit of a risk, wasn't he?"

"That's his style, as you know. He's always been a chancer. He was right, too. It paid off."

"But the Master found him."

"Yes, but he came in too late and he wasn't sharp enough. Or there may have been collusion. Or . . . I don't know. We never will exactly. *Apparently* the Master came in without Humphrey hearing him and he saw Humphrey reading the political theory paper. But what he didn't know was that Humphrey had already copied out the questions and stuffed the copy into his trouser pocket."

"Hmmm." Bognor pondered. It certainly explained a lot. Rook's pure alpha in political theory had been one of the most extraordinary results of the year. The oddest in modern history. "But," asked Bognor, "do you mean to say the Master let him go—just like that?"

"No, no, certainly not just like that. There was an enormous amount of agonising. Humphrey, naturally, swore blind that he'd hardly read any of the questions, hadn't realised what it was anyway, et cetera, et cetera, but the old boy wasn't daft. He saw through that one. On the other hand, what could he do?"

"He could have sent him down."

"With all the scandal. Bad for Humphrey, whom he liked. Bad for the college. Bad for him, being so careless. Bad all round."

"He could have set a new paper."

"He *could*. But remember, it was already in proof. It would have been an awful bore. Besides which, questions would have been asked. How could he have explained it away?"

Bognor shrugged. "So what did he do?"

"Well, as I say, he agonised for a bit and then he told Humphrey he'd have to think about it. After he thought about it he decided to do nothing, just let Humphrey off with a severe caution."

"And tell his father."

"Yes. And tell his father. Who couldn't have cared less as it happened. Boasted about it to *my* father, if you please. My father was the sort of man who cared very much, but that's by the way."

"All jolly interesting," said Bognor, "but I'm not absolutely crystal clear about the business of motive. Why should all this lead to Humphrey doing in the Master twenty years later?"

Molly blew smoke and gazed at him with affectionate

condescension. "You are adorable but you're fantastically dense," she said. "One of the reasons Lord Beckenham let him off with a caution was that he didn't think Humphrey had had the time to absorb very much. O.K.?"

"O.K."

"And he goes on believing this until the schools' results are out."

"Yes."

"At which point Humphrey produces this phenomenal result which can only mean one thing."

"Yes."

"Now"—Molly leaned forward and spoke very slowly and distinctly as if addressing an idiot child—"it is too late for the Master to accuse his pupil of cheating. In fact, if he were to do any such thing Humphrey would say that the Master had connived at it. In fact, he was all prepared to say that he had actually shown him the paper on purpose, by appointment, with malice aforethought."

"I see."

"So. What happens is that the Master has Humphrey in and says that he will let the matter rest, but that the secret remains and that if he feels that it is in the public interest to reveal it, then he would not shrink from doing so."

"Is that conjecture," asked Bognor, "or do you know for certain?"

"I know," said Molly, smiling guiltily. "I got it out of Humphrey in an unguarded moment, but I'm not going to go into all that."

"How much more do you know?"

"Oh, from here on in it's guesswork," she admitted, "but it's not difficult to guess. We know that unless something goes badly wrong Humphrey is shortly going to be adopted as the prospective candidate for Sheen Central. Right? As the Conservative candidate and hence the MP for life with all that that implies."

Bognor nodded again. It was beginning to make sense.

"All of which Lord Beckenham would consider as being

a matter of some concern to the public. And which has an added bite because his Lordship's old protégé has moved across from the extreme left to the far right. And as a life-long member of the Labour Party, Beckenham disapproves. Worse than that, he feels betrayed. He forgave Humphrey his Trotskyism because it was just the sort of youthful excess he would have liked to have indulged himself. Only he didn't have the guts."

"So you think Lord Beckenham was determined to scupper Humphrey's chances of becoming MP for Sheen." Bognor concentrated very hard on getting his thoughts into logical order. "And he used the only means at his disposal, namely, that Humphrey's cheating in his final exams."

"I didn't quite say that. And you don't have to prove either that he did or that he intended to—only that Humphrey *thought* he was going to."

"Ah." Bognor frowned at the remains of the amber liquid in his brandy balloon. "And you think he did? And murdered him to prevent it?"

"Yes."

"Bit far-fetched isn't it? For a born-again Christian."

"If you knew Humphrey like I knew Humphrey you wouldn't think it far-fetched. He wants to be a Member of Parliament more than anything else in the world."

Bognor shifted ground. Also his bottom. He had eaten too much and felt over-filled. Was drinking too much as well. Ought to stop. Probably wouldn't. No self-control, that was his trouble. But what in hell was the point of self-control? You were only young once and he wasn't any more. He had had youth, and he felt pretty let down by it. Hadn't someone once said that "youth was wasted on the young"? Wilde probably. Sort of thing Wilde was given to saying. Facile old pouf. Well as far as he was concerned, youth had not been wasted by him, misspent arguably, but not wasted. It was just not what it was cracked up to be. Middle age seemed likely to be equally disappointing, but

he had every intention and expectation of misspending
that too. Unlike Vole, Rook, Crutwell and Edgware.
"Let's have another brandy," he said dangerously.
Molly eyed him leerily. "Why not?" she agreed. "Too
late to mend my ways now."

By the time they returned to the Randolph, they were
quite tipsy and not much further on with the solution to
the crime. There was a motive for Rook, a motive of sorts,
but Bognor was too fuddled to be sure whether it was a
convincing motive or not. He had also been compelled to
admit that he was in Oxford to investigate the Master's
murder, and he had promised light-heartedly and light-
headedly to give the lady an exclusive when he finally got
his man, cousin Humphrey or not. But thoughts of murder
and detection had slipped his mind somewhere between
the second and third brandies, and as he ambled along the
street arm in arm with the femme fatale of the *Daily
Globe* he was aware mainly of her. She smelt rather nice,
and he was enjoying her proximity. Of course, she was
older than him and she had been around a bit, but he was
not averse to a little experience. A nightcap in the bar, and
then, who knew what might happen? She had had designs
on him before, and although they had never progressed beyond the drawing-board, Bognor was nothing if not easily
led. As he entered the vaulted foyer of the old hotel, therefore, his thoughts were mainly concupiscent. He had quite
forgotten that there was work still to do and he was quite
unprepared for the elongated figure in scarlet leathers who
rose up before him wagging its finger.

"At last," it said, "and about bloody time, too."

"What?" he said. For a moment he thought it was an
urgent telegram, but just as he was about to reach out for
the little yellow envelope which would contain some appalling news, probably from Parkinson, he realised that he
was being accosted by a Fellow of Apocrypha. "Oh," he
said, disengaging himself from Molly Mortimer.

"Well might you say, 'Oh,'" said Dr. Frinton. "I've been waiting in this wretched morgue for an age."

"Hello," said Molly, not in the least abashed, "I'm Mortimer of the *Globe*."

Hermione Frinton favoured her with a disdainful glance and returned to her prey.

"It's clearly after dinner," she said, "judging from your condition. You stink of garlic and booze." She sighed. "Too bad. I've brought you a helmet." And before either Molly or Bognor could do anything about it, she had thrust a white and silver bone dome into Bognor's unwilling hands and marched him reluctantly back into the night.

"Honestly," she said, in an exasperated voice, when they were outside, "I did expect a *little* professionalism from the Board of Trade. Bad enough to go out on the binge like that, but to go out with the press really is a bit steep."

"I was following up a lead," said Bognor, trying to sound haughty and self-righteous and realising to his chagrin that he was slurring his speech.

"Not good," said Hermione, "not good at all. Never mind, a quick spin on Bolislav will bring a rush of blood to the head. Reactivate the old grey matter."

"Bolislav?" Bognor was bewildered.

"Bolislav the Mighty. My favourite mediaeval monarch. Also my bike."

"Bike?"

"A Velocette. Last of the truly Great British bikes. Big, black and oily."

And, indeed, even as she spoke Bognor saw the machine in question parked rakishly on a double yellow line a few yards from the main entrance to the hotel. It looked, in the lamplight, almost live, like some supercharged beetle. Bognor swallowed hard.

"Those are your wheels?" he enquired, not even attempting to mask his petrified incredulity.

"What did you expect? A Metro?" She snorted through

those equine nostrils. "Hop on!" And she swung a drain-pipe leg across the saddle, grasped the handlebars and pushed the machine off its side stand. "You ride these things?" she called over her shoulder.

"Never," said Bognor, gritting his teeth. Gingerly he got on behind her as she kicked the starter and the bike immediately throbbed into action with a deep and prolonged farting from the silvery exhausts. Bognor was aware of a disturbing quantity of horsepower underneath him. Reluctantly he pulled the helmet down over his head and tried to buckle the strap.

"Hold tight," she instructed, shouting over the engine's beat, "and just move with me. Pretend we're dancing."

Bognor reflected that if they were to do that he'd be off in no time. Dancing was not his strong point. He was incapable of moving in time to either the music or his partner. He saw no reason why he should find motorcycling any different.

"Hold tight!" she shouted, and obediently he clasped her round the waist, though gingerly.

"Tighter than that! And bunch up closer."

He did as he was told, shut his eyes and said a quick prayer to St. Christopher. Then the machine jerked away from the curb, swung over at a forty-five-degree angle, righted itself and powered up to a red light, where it came to an abrupt but well-controlled halt. Bognor had shut both eyes at the first sign of motion, but now very gingerly he opened one and, peering over his chauffeuse's shoulder, observed the back gate of Balliol straight ahead. He clenched his fingers across Dr. Frinton's stomach and felt his paunch press against her back. The smell of motorcycle was very strong but his nose, tight against the nape of her neck, caught something more feminine, which lulled him a little.

The security was false and short-lived. Just before the light went green Dr. Frinton spurred Bolislav into flight again, cutting the right-hand bend, running through the

gears with an impressively staccato series of double de-
clutches and hugging the middle of the road with deadly
precision. Bognor had an empty feeling in the pit of his
stomach as if riding in a high-speed lift. The alcohol's an-
aesthetising effect had gone completely. He felt ill, frightened and not in the least exhilarated. He did not want to
die on a motorbike in the Cornmarket late at night. Messy.
Painful too, he would imagine. He tried to call out to Hermione to slow down but the words would not come. Besides, the Bolislav's din would have drowned all but the
most stentorian appeal. Dr. Frinton would have been like
something from Wagner if she hadn't been so thin. Well,
slim. Bognor kept both eyes closed, held on so tightly that
he felt as if he must be squeezing the life out of her, and
had no option but to sway in time to the bike. He tried to
numb his mind with thoughts of food, drink, sex, anything
to remove the fear and the torment, but nothing worked.
He prayed to St. Christopher and St. Jude and St. Doubt-
ing Thomas and bit his lips to stop himself screaming
until, quite without warning, the torture ceased.

"I said, 'Would you mind letting go?' We're here."

"What?" Bognor was not going to commit suicide.

"Unhand me, varlet. We've arrived." Hermione cut the
engine and Bognor felt the bone-shaking rhythm beneath
him die away. Reluctantly he relinquished his grasp on the
English tutor's waist and tottered backwards off the bike.

"I think I'm going to be sick," he announced weakly.

"Teach you to make a pig of yourself," said Hermione,
removing her bone dome and clipping it to side of the
bike. She shook her hair free and grinned. "You do look an
alarming shade of mint. Take your hat off."

Bognor gave an undignified lurch towards the wall of
Apocrypha, leaned against it, and belched. The release of
natural gases had a beneficial effect on his nausea but he
still felt grim.

"Oh, do pull yourself together!" Dr. Frinton removed
her gauntlets and unzipped her jacket a few inches, then

glanced up at the college coat of arms above the Great
Gate. "Great is Truth, and mighty above all things," she
recited. "We have work to do and you're shirking it. Come
on. The Board of Trade expects—"

Bognor flapped a hand at her in a pathetic gesture of
dismissal. "You go and look at the files. I'll stay out here
and get a bit of fresh air."

"Certainly not," she snapped. "You're coming with me.
This is a team effort. Now listen. I'm going over to Waldy
Mitten's rooms to get the keys to the Lodgings. By the
time I'm back I expect you to be in better shape." She
gave him an exasperated glare, relented slightly and ad-
vanced on him. "I said you should take your hat off," she
told him, unstrapping it herself and pulling it off his head.
"Put your head between your legs," she ordered, "like
this," and she grabbed the back of Bognor's neck and
thrust his head down to knee level. "Touch your toes!
Come on! One, two, three. One, two, three." She pumped
him up and down as if she were a PT instructor of the old
school. He began to feel dizzy.

"O.K.," she said, stopping. "Keep doing that until I get
back with the keys." And she marched off, swaggering.
Bognor cursed her under his breath, not daring to do so
aloud for fear of more of the same. Watching her retreat-
ing form, though, he was compelled to admit that, alarming and assertive and generally bloody though she could
be, she had astonishing legs. And motorcycling gear set
them off a treat. He belched again and stood upright and
unaided. It was time to take a grip on himself.

Ten minutes later, when she reappeared, he was back to
something approaching normal. She not only had the keys
but Mitten too. The Acting Master had come along to see
fair play.

Mitten was muttering: "Not altogether happy Hermione . . . rather irregular . . . I mean, I *am* in charge
. . . does put me in a somewhat embarrassing position

. . . really would prefer it if the Chief Inspector Chappie could be informed . . . I mean . . ."

"Oh, do stop wittering," said Dr. Frinton crisply. "I've got enough trouble with this inebriate from the Board of Trade without you being an old woman. Why can't everyone behave normally for a change?"

Mitten looked aggrieved but shut up all the same.

Hermione now turned on Bognor.

"You all right now?" she enquired with no evidence of sympathy.

"Perfectly," lied Bognor. "I'm just not used to being hurtled down the wrong side of the road at one hundred miles an hour on the back of a motor bike with a pretentious nickname."

"That's more like it." She tossed her head and glanced from one man to the other. All three were uncomfortably aware of the superiority of her sex.

"Right." She turned on an elegantly black booted heel, buckles clattering as she did. "*Vamos!* Let's see what's on the files."

The men followed somewhat sheepishly. Mitten was in a hairy, donnish tweed suit of the style he had worn on his visit to the Board of Trade. Office seemed to have made him pompous, stopped off that geyser of irreverence which had so endeared him to his pupils by exploding just when it was least expected and most needed, punctuating long-winded orations at college feasts and the pompous pretensions of world leaders come to collect their honorary degrees. Mitten was, paradoxically, diminished by his elevation. He was the poorer for power.

"Sold out," thought Bognor, as they followed the loping figure of Dr. Frinton along the ill-lit cloisters surrounding Tobit Quad. And yet it wasn't quite that. It was something more subtle and insidious. Possibly even sinister. Bognor couldn't put his finger on it.

"I'm not happy about this, Simon," said Mitten *sotto*

voce, as their leader increased her pace and outdistanced them by several yards. "She's so deucedly headstrong. Can she know what she's up to? And even if she does, is it right? I mean, I do think this sort of thing should be left to the professionals."

"She *is* a professional," snapped Bognor. "So am I," he added with less conviction.

"In a manner of speaking," conceded Mitten. "But there are professionals and professionals. I would prefer to be doing this rather more conventionally. I feel as if I'm Gordon Liddy."

"Well, you're not," said Bognor. "You're not even remotely like Gordon Liddy. You're acting on the side of law 'n' order. And justice. And all that sort of thing."

"That's what Nixon said," whispered Mitten miserably, as they passed out of the cloisters, through the Arch of the Maccabees, and into the Garden Quad, where they halted at the door of the Lodgings.

"O.K., Waldy, open up!" commanded Dr. Frinton.

Mitten reached in his pocket and pulled out a piece of wood to which two large old-fashioned keys were appended. The first did not fit, but the second did. Mitten turned it and the door creaked open. They were assailed by a smell of damp and decay. The place felt musty, as if its windows had been unopened for decades. Overlying this generalised aroma there were more specific scents. Bognor thought he detected very old fish, possibly stale milk. Perhaps cat droppings.

He wrinkled his nose and felt bilious again.

"Gosh!" he said. "Bit niffy, isn't it?"

Mitten took a polka-dot handkerchief from his breast pocket and waved it under his nose.

"Plumb's food," he said. "Scout hasn't cleared it out."

"We're not here to talk about the cat's breakfast," said Hermione. "This way," and she led them down the flagged hall, then left down a corridor to another locked door, which Mitten opened with the second key. He fumbled as he did so, irritating Dr. Frinton, who remarked that both the keys and locks were so old and primitive as to be quite pointless. Any eight-year-old with a piece of stiff card and a modicum of ingenuity could have broken in without the slightest problem. Bognor was about to protest that he personally found lock-picking an extraordinarily difficult art to master when the door did finally open and Hermione let out an ungrammatical sentence composed entirely of expletives which Bognor found surprisingly strong, even for her.

"Someone else had the same idea," said Bognor, following her into the room and eyeing the open filing cabinets and the scattered papers. The burglar had been messy.

"What makes you say that?" asked Mitten, gaping at the papers. He looked both perplexed and outraged. This was more than an ordinary burglary, it was an affront to the college. That was what his manner suggested.

"Simon's right," said Hermione. She bent down and scooped up a sheaf. "Putney, Earl of," she intoned. "Unpromising material but enough means to compensate. Gamma minus academically. Moral behaviour ditto . . ." She cast the sheet aside. "Finkelbaum, Ephraim. Outstanding intellect, but see involvement with ffrench-Winifred, Hubert." She threw that down too. "Butley, Basil, recommended to G for special work with Force Q on account of brilliant performance in rugger cuppers, also forceful leadership during anti-Fascist riots. See Dean's special report . . ."

"O.K.," said Bognor, "you've made your point." There was a cavernous, shiny leather armchair next to a large drooping aspidistra and Bognor sat down in it, heavily, sighed and passed a hand over a surprisingly sweaty brow.

"I presume he's got what we wanted?" he said. Hermione was on her hands and knees trying to sort through the former contents of the filing cabinets.

"Difficult to be certain," she said. "Everything's such a mess. He used to file by year with a complicated cross-reference system to moral tutors and coded indexes. He half-explained it to me once but it was so abstruse I think he'd forgotten it himself." She got to her feet and began to examine the cabinets themselves. "Looks like it," she said forlornly. "No sign of your year at all, Simon. We can check it out more thoroughly in the morning, but I'm afraid our murderer's got away with some nicely incriminating evidence."

"Pity," said Bognor. "I should like to have seen my entry."

"That I doubt," said Mitten. "It would have made salutary reading. But that's by the way. I don't understand how this could have happened. I mean, who could have got in without us knowing?"

Hermione snorted. "Not exactly Fort Knox," she said. "Any half-wit could have picked these locks."

"But," protested Mitten, "you have to get in to the college in the first place. There's only one way in."

"Rubbish," said Bognor. "There are a hundred and one climbable drainpipes to my certain knowledge. And even if he did come through the main gate, those porters are always asleep or half cut. Or both."

"I don't think that's fair," Mitten pouted. "College security has always been very strict."

"Don't be absurd." Hermione ran long fingers through autumn gold hair. "Question is *who?*"

"Rook," said Bognor. "I'm almost positive Rook's file was dynamite. My information is that he only got his first because he snitched a look at the political theory paper weeks before it happened."

"He what?" Frinton and Mitten looked at him incredulously.

"He got hold of the political theory paper in advance of the exam. Found it in this very room, no less. Was surprised by the Master, who kept mum. Accessory after the fact."

"Not possible," said Mitten.

Hermione Frinton ignored him. "Why didn't you tell us before?"

"Before what?" Bognor treated the question rhetorically and continued at once. "I couldn't tell you before anything. I only found out this evening and you were so bloody anxious to get me on the back of that absurd velocipede of yours that there was no chance to say 'good evening' let alone provide you with new and exciting information. If only you hadn't been so unforgivably impetuous . . ."

"Good grief!" she exclaimed. "You mean to say this is some drunken tittle-tattle you've picked up over dinner with that raddled old floosie you came weaving home with just now? Do me a favour."

Bognor glared.

Hermione Frinton glared.

Waldegrave Mitten blinked from one to the other.

Finally Bognor said, in his most theatrical manner, "I've had a long day and I'm going home to bed. No, thank you, I don't want a lift. I would rather walk. I'll see myself out."

And he did.

CHAPTER 5

It did not take him long to walk back to the Randolph this time. Anger sped his steps, and evaporated his fatigue. He was extremely cross, not to say insulted. He objected to implications of incompetence no matter where they came from. In the case of Parkinson they were to be expected. Parkinson's disdainful misgivings were a cross to bear, a running sore with which he had just about learned to live. Monica's gentle teasing was founded on friendship, even love, or so he believed. But this was quite different. A brand-new colleague accusing him of unprofessional conduct in front of his old tutor. And not any old brand-new colleague, but one he rather fancied. It was a bit much.

It was particularly thick because the more he thought about it the more suspicious Rook became. He had always been a flash Harry, too clever by half, always playing games with his friends' emotions and loyalties, playing a game with life itself, but not the sort of game Bognor wanted to join in with. Rook played like a professional, always calculating the next move, interested only in winning, not in taking part, happy to foul if it was necessary. Molly Mortimer's allegations were shocking, but, now that Bognor thought about them, entirely in character. Naturally Humphrey Rook would cheat. Who could have thought otherwise? The only real surprise was the Master's complicity, but Bognor could see how that had happened. To have shopped Rook at the time would have meant blackening his character and ruining his career. Beckenham would not have enjoyed that. It would have made him seem callous, particularly as part of the blame was his for leaving the exam paper lying around in such a careless manner. And Rook *was* a favourite son. It would have seemed much the easiest way out. Successful men, in Bognor's experience, always knew when to turn the blind eye. No reason to suppose that Beckenham was not perfectly Nelsonian in this respect.

If it hadn't been for his cheating, Rook would probably have got a third-class degree, just like Bognor. Had Bognor cheated, Bognor would, given Bognor's luck, have been found out. This thought made him still angrier, so that as he came swinging into the Randolph's lobby the fury was rising off him like steam. Even the most unobservant and casual bystander would have noticed that they were in the presence of a very angry man indeed.

Nor did his rage abate as he ascended to his room. Had it not been for Molly Mortimer he might have been heading bedwards with Hermione Frinton. Had it not been for Hermione Frinton he might have been heading bedwards with Molly Mortimer. This was, of course, the purest fantasy, for, despite his lascivious imaginings, Bognor never went to bed with anyone but the faithful Monica. Nevertheless, in matters of sex as in practically everything else Bognor was a fantasist, and as he moved towards a solitary bed in the cavernous hotel he found the prospect not so much depressing as enraging. In other bedrooms about the place there would, he knew full well, be endless energetic and adulterous couplings, regretted at breakfast perhaps, but not in the act. There, but for the grace of God, went he. Dammit!

So cross was he, and, of course, not yet sober that he fumbled with his key in the door and was unable to open it for a full thirty seconds. He was also insufficiently himself to notice that the light was on. Even if he had noticed he would merely have assumed that he had left it on before going out. He had no memory for such trivia at the best of times (which this, indubitably, was not) and would never have recalled his scrupulous switching off of lights immedi-

ately before meeting Molly in the bar. If he had, he would
probably have assumed that the chambermaid had left it
on while turning down his bed and so he would have been
just as unsuspecting as, in fact, he was. So that under no
circumstances would he have avoided the blow which
caught him sharply and adroitly on the back of the head as
he finally effected an entry to his room.

He slept soundly but dreamt vividly until shortly before
five o'clock. The dreams were confused but exciting. In all
of them he was being chased, though the identity of the
pursuer was not always clear. Often the chase was proces-
sional. He would be racing across some windswept moor,
with Professor Aveline bicycling behind him and gaining
by the yard. Behind the professor came Molly Mortimer
on horseback and behind her Hermione Frinton on Bolislav. Behind them, the Chief Inspector, Parkinson and
Waldegrave Mitten in an open Mercedes of the type
favoured by Goering. Behind them, Monica, armed with a
machine gun, flying through the air like Wonder Woman
with some mechanised hang-gliding contrivance strapped
to her torso. In other dreams he was hunted by Vole, Crutwell, Edgware and Rook, the four of them baying for him
like hounds after fox. He was always being pursued, except
for one particularly vivid dream, a replay of his oldest and
least favourite, the nightmare in which he was once again
forced to sit all thirteen papers of his final examinations at
Oxford. Decked out in "subfusc" of gown and white bow-
tie, he faced the ordeal with a mind of complete blankness,
an impenetrable fog of ignorance, which led to his hand-
ing in papers without a word written on them. It was a
peculiarly dreadful dream and in this version it culminated
in a horrific interview with Lord Beckenham, flanked by
Mitten and Aveline, attended by Vole, Crutwell, Edgware
and Rook. Lord Beckenham was wearing the full rig of a
Lord Justice, complete with wig, and after an interminable
catalogue of various awfulnesses, he finally donned a black
cap and announced with dire solemnity: "It is therefore

the sentence of this court that you be taken from this place and hanged by the neck . . ." At which point Bognor woke, bathed in sweat and shouting. He was lying on the carpet. For a moment he experienced that shock of complete disorientation which one always experiences when one wakes in a strange place.

He was so confused that for a joyous instant he was even under the impression that he felt quite well. But when he tried to move he realised that he was not only damaged but damaged fore and aft. Part of the pain was self-inflicted, the chemical consequence of excess alcohol ingestion. Bearable in isolation, but not when taken in tandem with the physical assault inflicted by whatever outside agency had hit him on the skull with a blunt object. It was one thing to have a hammering sensation *inside* the head; it was another thing to have a hammering sensation on the *outside* of the head; but it was something of an altogether different dimension when one was being hammered inside and out. He decided to lie very still and see if he could collect his thoughts. Such as they were.

"Hangover," he said to himself, hoarsely and out loud. Dimly he remembered the cognac. And the wine. And the Scotch. But if this was a hangover, then why was he lying in the middle of the carpet? He frowned and wished immediately that he had not. Frowning was agony. Hangovers were an occupational hazard of the Bognor life and as such they were instantly recognisable. Nor was drink on its own enough to floor him. It was ages since he had passed out from boozing. Not for, oh, twenty years or more. In fact, he couldn't remember keeling over from alcohol since that time after the Arkwright and Blennerhasset dinner when he had drunk the bottle of port. He smiled at the memory and let out a shrill gasp of anguish. Consider the corpse on the carpet, he mused, he frowns not, neither shall he smile. Better dead than this. Very gingerly he moved his right hand to the top right-hand corner of his head and tried touching it. Not a good idea. The merest dab produced an appalling sensation as if a demon acupuncturist was playing darts with his scalp.

It was then that the telephone sounded. It made him jerk violently as if he had shocked himself on a faulty piece of electrical wiring. This induced a wracking spasm of pain and each subsequent ring sent further slashing knife strokes into his defenceless brain. It was no good just lying there on the floor, much as he wanted to. It would, he knew, be agonising to get to his feet and blunder across to the telephone, but the searing rings of the instrument had a horribly insistent sound. They were not going to go away, and if he went on lying on the floor he would shortly expire. If he made a dash for it, death might well ensue, but death would at least come swiftly.

He inhaled deeply, braced himself for the effort and lunged across the room towards the offending shrill, succeeded in lifting the receiver from its cradle and put it to his ear, expecting to hear the voice of his unloved boss. For once he was wrong. It was not Parkinson who spoke. It was Smith.

"Is that Simon Bognor?" To Bognor's tortured hearing Smith's voice sounded alarmingly gloomy.

"Yes," he croaked, "Simon Bognor speaking." Each syllable hurt.

The policeman's voice seemed to falter.

"Are you all right?" he asked, a barely discernible note of sympathy twanging over the wires.

"No." Bognor considered expanding on this, but decided against it. Words equalled effort equalled acute discomfort. He had been kneeling by the bed up until this moment and now hauled himself to his feet and succeeded in sitting down on it. As he did, he let out a moan of anguish.

"Bognor? You there? You all right?"

Bognor gritted his teeth and tried speaking through them. "No. Half dead. Someone tried to kill me."

The Inspector swore. "I'm sending a car round," he said.

"What, now?" Bognor wanted to sleep. Die, even. Mind and body screamed out for oblivion.

"In ten minutes. They'll be with you by four at the latest."

"Four?!" Bognor groaned. "A car at four in the morning?"

Smith sounded relentless, no trace of compassion now. Perhaps he suspected a hangover, or some form of hallucination.

"It's necessary, I'm afraid. Can't say too much over the phone. And stay out of trouble. Don't answer the door to anyone except my men. I don't want a third death on my hands. Not before breakfast."

"A *third* death?"

"Ten minutes," said the Inspector. "I'll see you later." And he snapped down the receiver and cut off the line with a brutal finality which Bognor, eyes closed, could visualise all too easily. Trouble, trouble, trouble, he moaned to himself. He sat, slumped on the bed, and tried to work out who could be dead. It was a distressing tendency in Bognor's cases for a second death to follow a first within hours or at least days of his beginning enquiries. His natural and strong inclination was to maintain that this was simply coincidence. Nevertheless, he had read his Koestler and had enough natural scepticism to be worried by persistent coincidence. He had to confess, at least to Monica and himself, that coincidence was a facile explanation. This was something worse. It had, he was very much afraid, something to do with cause and effect.

He had seldom felt worse. Fruitless to catalogue those occasions which might compete. In the past he had nearly always had the opportunity to sleep off the worst of this kind of disaster, but now he was to be jerked untimely from his sleep and forced to contemplate a corpse. Thank heaven, he had remembered the Alka-Seltzer. It was on the glass shelf above the wash-basin, and with another superhuman effort he staggered to it and switched on the fluorescent strip light above the shaving mirror. A mistake. The face that blinked back at him was a deeply distressing apparition. Blood had run down one side and stained the skin. His hair around the temple was clotted with the stuff and tufts of carpet adhered to his cheek and chin. Apart from the dried red blood, some broken veins and the odd pimple his face was a drained yellow colour. Seeing such a face on another man's body Bognor would have crossed the road and passed by on the other side. As it was, he squinted at it through half-closed, puffy-lidded eyes. There was nothing he could say about it, he decided after a moment's frantic contemplation, and so, very carefully in order not to jerk and thereby risk further harm, he decanted a handful of white Alka-Seltzer tablets into a glass of water. Leaving them to fizz for a few seconds, he turned the cold tap on full blast and, still moving with the deliberation of a man on his penultimate legs, he lowered his head into the basin and let it remain there, sighing spasmodically as the cold water splashed about it. Eventually he straightened and quaffed the Alka-Seltzer, trying not to look himself in the eye. Then, thinking that perhaps he was feeling marginally less ghastly, he ventured a glance at the image in the glass. Less blood than before, but otherwise enough to turn the least squeamish stomach. He pulled at the knot of his Arkwright and Blennerhasset tie, then dabbed at the blood with a dampened face towel. His head under the hair was still leaking, but the blood which must have flowed quite freely at first was now merely oozing. Everything still hurt like hell, but before long the Alka-Seltzer might take some of the edge off the damage. He wondered if he needed stitches. Probably. Would he be able to stay conscious? Perhaps. Who was the second corpse? Molly Mortimer? Hermione Frinton? Waldy Mitten? Maybe an Apocryphal scholarship candidate, thwarted by the examining body, was going to knock off the Senior Common Room one by one. Oh, for Codes and Ciphers! Oh, for home and Monica! If the police were going to be ten minutes arriving, he might just have time for a quick lie-down . . . He made his way back to the bed and sprawled on it, face down.

He was awoken immediately, though so deep was the oblivion to which he succumbed as soon as his head touched the counterpane, that he felt as if he had been asleep for weeks. The banging on the door provoked a dream at first, and waking, Bognor was surprised to find himself protesting in Shakespearean tones he had not used since his last term at school: "Knock, knock, knock! Who's there, in the name of Beelzebub?"

At which there was a pause before a voice, at once officious and subordinate, shouted back, "Police, sir. Constable Atkinson. Come from Inspector Smith."

Bognor frowned. The Inspector had said he was sending a car round, but he had also warned Bognor against opening the door to any but his own men. How could he know whether this Constable Atkinson was the real thing, or the failed assassin returned to finish the job off properly?

"Who do you want?" asked Bognor cautiously.

"Mr. Bognor of the Board of Trade, sir. Is that you, Mr. Bognor?"

Bognor's head throbbed. This was silly. "Look," he said, "even if it is me, your Inspector Smith warned me not to let anyone in except you. If you are you. Do you have any ID?"

Another pause, a shuffling, a rustling and then the sound of someone fiddling with the bottom of the door. A moment later a plastic-coated card slid underneath it and lay on the carpet.

"ID, sir," said the voice. "I think you'll find it in order."

Bognor knelt, not without difficulty and discomfort, and managed to scoop the card off the floor. It revealed, as expected, that its owner was, as had been suggested, Detective Constable Atkinson of the local CID. Bognor accordingly opened up to find himself staring at a burly red-faced man with bushy eyebrows, a Donegal tweed jacket, grey flannel trousers and brown brogues. On seeing Bognor, this worthy took two smart steps back and removed his hands from his pockets.

"Crippen!" he exclaimed, evidently using the famous murderer's name as an expression of astonishment. He did not seem to Bognor to be suggesting that he *was* Crippen, nor even that Bognor was a latter-day victim of the doctor. It was simply an expletive. Bognor smiled weakly, glad of creating such an instant and dramatic effect. It did not often happen. In fact, quite often he was not noticed at all until things started to go wrong and Parkinson produced him as a scapegoat. The smile was not much of a success. Scarcely worth the effort.

"Stone the crows!" continued the constable. "What you been doing?"

Bognor indicated his head, dabbing at the wound, just above the temple. His fingers came away bloody and he gazed at them thoughtfully for a moment before showing them to the policeman.

"Jesus," said Constable Atkinson, glancing rapidly to left and right, and at the same time slipping a hand to his hip and producing an ugly black revolver. With his other hand he pushed Bognor back into the room. Once inside, he replaced the gun and examined Bognor's injury. "That's not at all nice, sir, if I might say so. Whoever did that was taking quite a risk, or he didn't know what he was about. Could have killed you, that could. Can you walk?"

"I can try," muttered Bognor.

"Ought to take you straight round to casualty," said Atkinson sympathetically. "Only I'm afraid that's a little luxury the Chief isn't going to allow us." He looked at his watch. "Donner und Blitzen," he said unexpectedly, "We're late as it is. We've got a first-aid kit in the car. I'll find something to put on it even if it's only some antiseptic and a strip of Band-Aid. Who did it? Any idea?"

"None," said Bognor ruefully, "Jumped me the second I opened the door."

Atkinson glanced round the room. "Looking for something," he said, gesturing towards the drawers and cupboards, all of which were open.

Bognor simply had not noticed. Even now he was not sure whether the whirlwind effect, the scattered clothing, the ransacked drawers, the confetti of papers was the result of interlopers or of his own untidiness.

"Any idea what?"

"What what?"

"What they were looking for?"

"None. Nor who."

"Who?"

"Yes, who. Who hit me on the head. No idea who."

"Oh." Atkinson rubbed his chin and stared around him at the debris. "Anything missing?" he asked.

"Dunno," said Bognor, truthfully but unhelpfully.

Atkinson glanced at him sharply and decided that this was best pursued at some later date. "Maybe some brandy in the car" he said pleasantly.

"Ugh." Bognor retched and shuddered. "Anything but brandy," he said.

The Detective Constable frowned. "Best be going, sir, if you can manage it."

Bognor told him, unconvincingly, that he could manage perfectly well, but after a few steps it was clear that he needed official support, so that they made most of the journey arm in arm and passed through the lobby like a couple in post-coital euphoria, causing the hall porter to raise his eyebrows, suck his teeth, shake his head and observe, *sotto voce*, that he didn't know what the place was coming to and that young gentlemen had ceased being young gentlemen many years ago.

Outside, the white police Rover was parked on the double yellow line, engine running, blue light flashing. Atkinson guided Bognor into the back seat, then got in alongside the driver. The car shot forward like a hound from the traps, ramming Bognor's stomach against his spine.

"Oh, well," he gasped as he slumped into the upholstery, "better than Bolislav."

"I beg your pardon, sir?" Atkinson turned, sympathetically. He had found the first-aid kit and was rummaging about in it, searching for sticking plaster.

"Motor bike," said Bognor, grinning queasily. "I was on one earlier. Took the breath away."

Atkinson smiled uneasily. "I see, sir. Now, if you wouldn't mind just leaning forward a bit, I'll have a go at cleaning up that cut and sticking something over it."

But even as he said it Bognor's eyes closed, his mouth fell open and he slipped away into the release of sleep. Atkinson regarded him briefly to see if he was breathing, was reassured by the onslaught of stentorian snores and turned back to face the front.

"Not in a good way, poor sod," he said to his colleague.

"What happened to him?"

"Had a skinfull, went home to bed and got hit on the head with a blunt instrument. Not so blunt it didn't cut him, though. Table lamp probably, unless whoever done it was carrying a cosh. Amateur, whoever it was. Messy."

They drove on in silence, speeding along the deserted road through North Oxford, along the bypass, turning off on a minor road and then, still travelling at a reckless clip which would have terrified Bognor had he been awake, they passed through a trio of dormant picturesque country villages of the type favoured by week-enders from London and the richer, trendier Oxford dons. In a fourth, even more picturesquely post-card than the others, they turned left by the church and down a lane which, after a mile or so, became little more than a muddy track. They climbed for a few minutes, rattled over a cattle grid and parked a hundred yards further on where several vehicles already stood and where the night was illuminated by lights and torches. As they halted, the bemackintoshed figure of Inspector Smith was caught in the beam of the headlights, and Bognor woke.

His first coherent vision was of the Inspector easing into the rear seat alongside him.

"Bad business," he said.

Bognor did not reply.

"Anyway, can't be helped. Just to have to hope there's a silver lining. How are *you?*" He snapped on the interior light and caught his breath as he saw Bognor properly. "Sorry I asked," he said after a moment. He felt in the pocket of his mac and pulled out a hip flask. "Here," he said, "brandy. You look as if you could use it."

Bognor gagged and turned his head away.

"Suit yourself," said the Inspector, taking a swig himself before putting the flask back in his pocket. "So someone had a go at you, eh?"

Bognor nodded.

"Any idea who?"

Bognor shook his head.

"When did this happen?"

Bognor said he couldn't be sure, but it must have been between eleven and twelve. Or so he supposed. The Inspector nodded at this and gave an impression of thought. When he had finished he said, "Perfectly possible for whoever did for our friend over there to have got back in time to have a go at you too."

"When . . . ?" began Bognor, then checked himself. "I mean, *who* was it?"

"Time of death estimated at somewhere around seven or eight yesterday evening," replied Smith, "in answer to the first part of your question. As for the second, you'd better come and have a look. He hasn't been moved yet, and the only identification so far is from his driving licence and credit cards. Since he was a friend of yours, you'd better do the honours. Can you walk?"

"Up to a point."

"It's not far."

They both got out of the car and Bognor stood for a second testing the springy upland turf.

"Bit of luck finding him this quick," said Smith conversationally. "This couple came up for a quick spot of how's your father and just fell over him. Bad luck on them, I'm afraid. Both of them playing away from home, if you know what I mean. Not that there's anything unusual about that in this day and age. There'll be trouble, though. University types they were. Told their respective spouses they were going to choir practice. Ha!" He laughed coldly. "The Almighty moves in mysterious ways, his wonders to perform, don't you think?"

There was a heavy dew underfoot and it soaked through Bognor's suedes, moistening his socks. To his already frightful physical condition he now added a driness of the throat and a tightening of the stomach. Something to do with apprehension. Collecting his thoughts was out of the question. He could not even begin to guess whose body was lying out here on the hillside, stumbled upon by an adulterous courting couple. What a way to go. For himself, he wanted to die in bed, preferably at once.

Some sort of bivouac had been placed over the dead person, and as they reached it Smith pulled aside the end and shone his torch in, illuminating the man's face. Bognor, braced for the shock, stared in, gulped, swallowed hard and turned away. Smith caught him as he half-fell and forced some of the contents of his flask down his throat. This time Bognor was almost grateful for it, but after taking it he broke away from Smith and took a few steps into the darkness. He wanted to be alone, and for a short while the policeman granted the unspoken wish. Then, all too soon, he was at his elbow again.

"Sorry about that," he said, "Friend of yours, was he?"

"It's not that," said Bognor. "Only, I'm afraid, that in a manner of speaking it's my fault. I should have bloody well listened. Damn! Damn! Damn!" He pulled out a spotted handkerchief and blew his nose loudly.

"The documents," said Inspector Smith, "lead us to suppose that the deceased is one Sebastian Vole."

"Yes," said Bognor softly, "that's Vole all right."

CHAPTER 6

Bognor sat on the back seat of the Rover with his head between his knees and moaned softly. It was idle to pretend that he had ever numbered the dead man among his nearest and dearest, but their acquaintanceship went back to days of callow youth, wine and roses, salad, carefree this and that and what have you. And that meant something. Bognor did not exactly weep for Vole, but he did allow himself a little stiff-upper-lipped keening. Of all his contemporaries, Vole was the only one who remembered Christmas. Every year the card came without fail: "Season's Greetings from Prendergast History Faculty," and, in green ink, the spikily executed words "Sebastian Vole." Of all his brilliant contemporaries, Vole had been the most—well—human. Vole stayed up all night playing poker. Vole liked a drink. Vole had been sick over the Junior Proctor one night after an Arkwright and Blennerhasset meeting. Vole was all right. And now, alas, poor Vole, he lay stiff and cold on an Oxfordshire hillside. This *had* been a professional job. Hands tied, blindfolded. A single shot from close range in the back of the neck.

"It's my fault," moaned Bognor again. "If only I'd listened."

Smith, who was standing outside, leaning against the open window, sympathised with his colleague's pain and grief but was becoming bored by this incomprehensible refrain. Now that he had heard it half a dozen times, he decided he could seek elucidation without seeming callous.

"What was it," he asked kindly, "that he told you?"

"About his book," moaned Bognor. "He was right all the time. Just because he made such an ass of himself with

Mussolini, I didn't believe him. But he was right. Dammit, he was right, and look where it got him. Shot in the back by that Kremlin sociologist. God, this country's going to the dogs!"

The Inspector took another swig from his flask and frowned. He had lost the thread of his colleague's remarks. "Come again," he said helpfully. "I'm not quite with you."

"We *all* mocked him," said Bognor, "but *he* was right and *we* were wrong."

"But what did he tell you?"

"He told me he was on to Professor Aveline."

"What, *the* Professor Aveline? Professor *Max* Aveline? The Regius Professor of Sociology?"

"The same."

The Inspector cleared his throat noisily. An ambulance had arrived. They were taking Vole away. Bognor watched in the grey half-light of early morning. There was a damp mist shrouding the hillside. The men's breath steamed. He was reminded of the last dawn he had seen, no time at all ago, the morning after the Gaudy, the morning Lord Beckenham walked home to his death. And now Vole.

"And what do you mean when you say he was 'on' to Aveline? You're too quick for me, I'm afraid. I'm only a poor policeman. Don't have the benefits of a varsity education like you."

Bognor didn't like people who said varsity. It reminded him of Betjeman:

I'm afraid the fellows in Putney rather wish they had
The social ease and manners of a "varsity undergrad."

And thinking of Betjeman, Bognor remembered another of the Laureate's verses, bleaker lines on the death of some old Fellow of Pembroke:

The body waits in Pembroke College where the ivy
taps the panes
All night.

and then:

> Those old cheeks that faintly flushed as the port
> suffused the veins,
> Drain'd white.

Beckenham, Vole . . . no more port for either of them. Both drained whiter than white. Vanished as if they had never been. Would Vole's manuscript be published after death? Could you be awarded a posthumous All Souls' Fellowship? Would justice be done? And seen to be done?

"I hate to hurry you." The policeman meant the exact opposite of what he said. Chivvying people along was what he liked best in all the world. If Bognor had been a suspect and not a colleague he might have hit him about a bit in the cause of truth. The thought passed through both men's minds.

"Sorry," said Bognor, not meaning it either. "I had a long talk with Vole yesterday. He made me promise not to say anything about it for forty-eight hours."

"As the result of which . . ." said the Inspector. Unnecessarily, Bognor thought.

"It was supremely important to him," he snapped. "You could say that his life's work depended on it."

"Life too, come to that."

"Yes. Well."

Another protracted silence ensued and then Bognor told Inspector Smith about his conversation with Vole. Smith did not comment until the story was complete, and even then he waited while he dragged out a battered briar pipe, stuffed it full of shag and lit it clumsily.

"Can't say," he said at last, between spluttering puffs. "I'm surprised you took it with a pinch of salt. Not a likely story."

"That's what I thought," said Bognor. "If this were Cambridge, it would be different, but I've always assumed that sort of thing couldn't happen here."

"So you're saying Aveline tied him up, blindfolded him, shot him and then drove out here and dumped him?"

Bognor pondered. Aveline may have been amazingly virile for his age but his age was considerable. It seemed unlikely that he could have dealt so effectively with even a drunken Vole.

"He'd have needed help."

"And," Smith blew a cloud of Auld Reekie in Bognor's direction, "you're thinking what I'm thinking."

"Which is?" Bognor was not going to be caught out like that.

"That is, he's who Vole thought he was, then he'd know precisely where to go for that sort of help."

"Quite."

"Next question is, can we prove it?" The Inspector puffed away thoughtfully.

"Don't see why not," said Bognor. "If Vole left all his notes and working papers at Prendergast, that should give us enough evidence to smoke Aveline out. Besides, if he really was working for the Russians all these years, someone must have had *some* sort of an idea."

"I wouldn't bet on it," said Smith. "Anyway, I think we should strike while the iron's hot. Almost time for breakfast. Let's take a coffee and some toast off the Regius Professor."

Smith slid into the back seat alongside Bognor, who, on the point of vomiting, asked him to extinguish the pipe. He did, and the car moved away down the hill some five minutes behind the ambulance carrying Vole's corpse to the mortuary. There was a phone box in the village and Smith decided they should stop there to find Aveline's address in the directory. When they got there, however, they discovered that the phone book was missing.

"I'll try Directory Inquiries," said Smith, asking Bognor for a 10p coin. Bognor had no such thing, so walked to the car and borrowed one from Constable Atkinson. When he got back he said, "He's bound to be ex-directory. No point trying. I'll call Waldegrave Mitten. He'll know." He glanced at his watch, which showed him it was not long after six. It would be satisfying to telephone Mitten at this ungodly hour. He was certain to be asleep, having no more love for the early morning than Bognor himself.

It took him no little time to persuade the college porter of the importance of his request, but eventually he was put through to the acting Master's rooms. The bell rang several times before an aggrieved, strangulated voice said, "Do you know what bloody time it is?"

"About six-fifteen, actually," said Bognor. "But it *is* important. Very. I'm afraid we've had another death."

"Who is this?"

"Bognor," said Bognor, "Bognor, Board of Trade. That *is* Waldegrave Mitten, isn't it?"

"Oh, it's you," said Mitten with an air of resignation. "Could you ring back in an hour. It's not, er, convenient."

"Convenience doesn't come into it." Bognor spoke with asperity. "I need Aveline's address. There's been another death."

"If Aveline's dead, you hardly need his address."

"Aveline's not dead. It's someone else. I can't talk about it on the phone."

"You're not making sense," protested Mitten. "In fact, you sound like one of your essays. If someone else is dead, why do you need Aveline's address?"

"Listen," said Bognor, "this is not something I can talk about over the phone, but I do assure you it's vital. Please, may I have Aveline's address."

"He has a flat in Norham Gardens," said Mitten, "but I happen to know he's not there."

Bognor sighed. "I've only got one 10p piece," he said, "and we're going to run out of time in a moment. I'm not at all well, a man is dead and I must know where Professor Aveline is."

"He's at his cottage," said Mitten, "but I can't give you the address. He's most particular about it. It's his hideaway. He'd kill me if I gave it to you."

"Since he's killed at least one man already, I should

think that's very much on the cards," said Bognor drily. "You don't seem to realise we're investigating a murder. Two murders, in point of fact. You're obstructing us in our enquiries. That's an offence."

Mitten was manifestly exasperated, but after some ritual huffing, puffing and minatory muttering he did say, "Oh, very well then, but I want you to know that I do this under protest. Also, that under no circumstances are you to tell Max how you found out."

"No, no, of course not. Just tell me where it is."

A pause. "The Old Bakehouse, Compton Courtenay. It's about ten miles outside Oxford."

"Thanks very much," he said. "You can go back to sleep now." And he replaced the receiver noisily.

"Compton Courtenay," he said to the Inspector, squeezed up against him in the kiosk.

"Ah," said the Inspector, a glint coming into the eyes. "Now that *is* a piece of luck."

Bognor caught a heavy whiff of armpit, whisky and stale tobacco. Quickly he opened the door and tumbled out.

"Luck?" he enquired from the soggily bracing safety of the great outdoors.

"Luck, laddie. Look," and he jabbed a finger at the code on the dial. "Compton Courtenay 2246 X," he said triumphantly. "We're in bloody Compton Courtenay already."

"Oh," said Bognor, "that *is* good news. All we have to do now is find the Old Bakehouse. Then we can sit down and have a jolly little breakfast with Mad Max the Murderous Marxist."

"Sorry," said the Inspector. "Forgot you were feeling a degree or two under. You want to get stitched up and have a kip? Nothing much you can do at the moment, and I can get a car to drive you into casualty at the Radcliffe."

"No, thanks," said Bognor. "Let's go and collect the Professor first. Always assuming he's still there. Are you armed?"

Smith nodded. "Atkinson and the others too. He jerked his head towards the second car, which was stopped just outside the Belt and Braces public house.

"Not that you need to worry about that," he went on. "If he did murder your friend Vole, the odds are that he'll have scarpered. On the other hand, if he's still in bed, then he's innocent."

"That sounds a bit simple," said Bognor. "How do you work that out?"

"Common sense, experience, and a feel for the job," said Inspector Smith, managing to suggest that these essential qualifications were not shared by his colleague from the Board of Trade. "Come on! Let's go. Aren't more than about a dozen houses to choose from."

This was correct. A hundred years ago and more this would have been a small feudal village owned by the local lord and peopled by his tenants and workers. Now, however, the local lord was reduced to living in the west wing while the paying public had the run of the rest of the house. The workers were all in council estates on the edge of Oxford or Thame. The only people who lived in Compton Courtenay were Regius Professors of Sociology and Company Directors. The Regius Professor's abode was the third house they came to, a ducky little stone and thatched number with roses and honeysuckle round the porch, staddle-stones by the front path, heavily leaded windows and a strong suspicion of *House and Garden* exposed beam and Aga. Very Volvo and Brie, as the Americans would have it.

Bognor, unarmed as usual, lurked in the background, nursing his wounds, aches and self-recrimination, while the constabulary fanned out to cover all possible entrances and exits. Smith, as befitted the man in charge, made purposefully for the front door and knocked on it three times loudly with the heavy iron knocker. There being no answer, he tried again. After a third effort he took out a hand-gun, motioned two policemen to cover him, and turned the door handle. The door opened. Standing back, the Inspector gave it a kick, and waited. Bognor, watching, decided that his colleague chappie was more nervous than he liked to admit.

The early morning silence was broken by the church clock striking the quarter. The door, under the impact of the Inspector's kick, swung wide open and then, very slowly and with a slight creak, swung back. The Inspector pushed it open with his hand this time and entered. Behind him followed the two policemen. Bognor, for reasons he preferred not to examine (they would have had too much to do with extreme caution, not to say fear), remained outside. About five minutes later the Inspector emerged.

"Done a bunk," he shouted. "Come on in. The other two are making coffee."

Bognor did as he was asked, feeling too like a trespasser for comfort. He wiped his feet fastidiously on the mat and found himself in a long, low living room with stairs leading to the upper storey. Two rooms and a passage had obviously been knocked into one. By the surprisingly chintzy high-backed armchairs there were empty glasses and two ashtrays with several butts in them. The grate contained ash. Yesterday's *Guardian* lay open on a window seat and on the dining table at the far end of the room a cut glass jug half full of water sat next to a bottle of Dimple Haig whisky with about an inch left in the bottom. The room smelt faintly pub-like, tobacco and alcohol mixing with more animal smells. Although it was messy, there were no signs of a struggle.

The Inspector rubbed his hands together, making a rasping sound with the palms. "Done a bunk," he said again, "Shaving things missing from the bathroom. Drawers opened. Left in a hurry. Didn't even wash up or lock behind him."

"People don't lock front doors in the country."

"Call this country?" said the Inspector sceptically. "Should be prints on the glasses. Neighbours may have noticed something." Constable Atkinson appeared bearing hot Nescafé in Portmeirion pottery mugs. Bognor shovelled three spoonfuls of sugar into his and drank it black.

"Open and shut," he said.

"Oh, yes." The Inspector cocked an eyebrow. "Enlighten me."

"O.K." Bognor took a deep breath. "Vole has all the evidence necessary to prove that Aveline was the Kremlin's top Briton. Made Philby look like an office boy, were his words, if I remember correctly. So he asks Aveline for an interview. Aveline naturally knows that Vole's been on the trail for years and he realises that he's finally caught up with him. He has to make sure, of course. He knows Vole didn't really do his homework on the Mussolini book so there's a chance he's been careless again. But Aveline is worried." Bognor sipped the sickly sweet brew and mopped his forehead. He wondered if he should bother to get his wound stitched. "So rather than risk exposure in the twilight of his days," he continued, "he gets onto his friends and asks them to send up one of their high-powered heavies to help him out if things go wrong. Vole arrives, slightly pissed. Boris sits in on the interview. It very quickly becomes apparent that Vole knows chapter and verse, so Boris pulls a gun, trusses poor old Vole up like poultry and bundles him away to a quiet spot where he shoots him and dumps him. Meanwhile Aveline, as you put it, does a bunk and Boris goes back to Millionaires Row, where he doubtless masquerades as a third secretary —cultural."

"Yes." Smith seemed weary. "I'll buy that as far as it goes. In which case, Aveline could be in Moscow by now. Though I'll put out a call just in case. He's probably had twelve hours and, with the resources at his disposal, any one of a number of passports. Trouble is, I don't see that any of this gets us any further."

"What do you mean . . .'further'?"

"I mean," said the Inspector, "that this murder enquiry

began with the death of Lord Beckenham of Penge. Am I right?"

"You are right."

"And we still don't know who did that."

"We don't?"

"*I* don't."

Bognor pursed his lips. "Beckenham was a stooge of Aveline's. One of what will, no doubt, turn out to have been a complex network of moles and agents and fifth-columnists. As soon as Beckenham was approached by Vole, he would have consulted Aveline. Aveline would have been worried that Beckenham would spill the beans, and so he knocks him off before Vole can get at him. QED."

"Several things wrong with that," said Smith. "One: lack of opportunity. How did he doctor the Master's raspberry tipple? He was in his own rooms all that night until he bicycled back to his flat in North Oxford. Two: he'd have been out here with Vole when the Master's filing cabinet was being done over. And three: he'd have been on his way to Moscow when you were being hit over the head at the Randolph. All of which adds up to quite conclusive evidence that, whatever else he may have done, Professor Aveline did not kill Lord Beckenham. Not QED at all."

"No. I suppose not. Except that he could have got someone else to do the dirty work. He got someone else to kill poor Vole."

"But he used a pro," said Smith. "Whoever knocked you about was an amateur. And so was the geezer who did the Master's files. If Aveline was the kind of operator you say he is, then he'd have had more class than that."

"So where does that leave us?" asked Bognor.

"Nowhere much," said the Inspector. "We'll follow this one through, naturally, but all we're going to find is that it was the Professor who did it, for reasons aforementioned, and that he's got clean away. If he didn't and if he hasn't, I'm a virgin."

Bognor nodded. "I wish he *had* done it," he said, "but I

agree. I don't think he did. And now, if you don't mind, I think I'd better get stitched up and have a quick kip."

It looked as if they were right. By the time Bognor surfaced, feeling weary but human, it transpired that Aveline, using his own name, had caught the night boat from Southampton to Le Havre. By the time the Inspector and Hermione Frinton had managed to get Interpol and the French security people to treat the matter with anything approaching seriousness, Aveline had vanished. This was hotly disputed by the French and some other European officials, who denied that in the latter half of the twentieth century it was possible for individuals simply to disappear into thin air. It was also claimed that border security was amazingly rigorous and foolproof. That even if the fugitive professor was able to elude the enveloping tentacles of the French dragnet, he would be snaffled the second he came within sight of the border. Bognor shrugged and sighed and wondered how long it would be before some watchful Western newspaper correspondent recorded a sighting of Aveline in the crush bar at the Bolshoi, or browsing in the Hermitage. Days, rather than weeks, in his opinion.

Vole's death and his own battering did have one happy side-effect, which was a reconciliation of sorts with Dr. Frinton. On waking in mid-afternoon, feeling revived and even marginally peckish, he sauntered down to the lounge in search of a pot of tea and a round or two of hot buttered toast. After ordering these, he checked with reception for messages (he had left the strictest imaginable instructions that he was under no circumstances whatever to be disturbed) and found, along with half a dozen increasingly angry messages from Parkinson, a note from Hermione, handwritten and presumably hand-delivered. It said: "Sorry about last night. Your gin is still in the fridge. Potter round as soon as you recover use of your limbs. Love, Hermione."

This perked him up no end, and after consuming tea

and toast with surprising enthusiasm he did indeed potter
round to Dr. Frinton's pad in Walton Street. He was disconcerted on arriving to find that the house appeared to be
given over to something called the International Vegan
Brotherhood for International Peace and Harmony. In a
scruffy ground-floor office a whey-faced man with long
pigtails and an unkempt beard streaked with green told
him that Dr. Frinton lived in the attic. Bognor ascended
the narrow staircase gingerly, for the carpet was threadbare
and only loosely attached to *terra firma*. Some way up, further progress was barred by a door. On the left-hand side
was a bell-push with the word Frinton. Bognor pressed it
and was rewarded by a metallic, disembodied but recog-
nisably Hermionian voice issuing from a grille above the
bell-push.

"Yes?" was all she said.

"It's me," said Bognor to the grille, "Simon Bognor of
the Board of Trade."

"Enter Simon Bognor of the Board of Trade. And bring
in the milk, if there's any there."

Bognor could see no milk. He pushed the door open and
climbed more narrow stairs, immaculately carpeted, this
time, in chocolate haircord. Seconds later he emerged into
an unexpectedly airy and almost enormous room in the
middle of which Dr. Frinton sat in the lotus position clad
only in an emerald-green leotard with the legend "All
Souls Yoga XV" across the chest. There was a strong smell
of joss-stick, and from the quadraphonic loudspeakers
there issued the clipped, desiccated and crackling voice of
T. S. Eliot reading *The Waste Land*.

"Oh," said Bognor backing off, "did I come at a bad
time?"

"Not in the least, darling," said Hermione, not moving
anything except her lips, and these no more than absolutely necessary for the purpose of speech. "Just having a
quick think."

"Ah," said Bognor. He wandered over to the plate-glass

windows which ran along the entire length of the room, giving onto an elegantly pot-planted terrace and affording inimitably Oxonian vistas of spires, dreaming.

"The fridge is in the kitchen," she said. "You should be able to recognise the gin. It has an olive in it."

"Thanks. I'll wait." Books did furnish the room. They did so somewhat ostentatiously, expensive coffee-table numbers jostling battered volumes from the London Library, almost certainly long overdue for return. Bognor picked up a copy of Cobb's *Tour de France* and tried to decipher the inscription, which was effusive, not easily decipherable and evidently from the author himself. Bognor's French was not up to it so that he discarded it and instead gazed out of the window across the Oxford landmarks to the great green dome of Apocrypha itself. Who would have thought, all those years ago, that he would return to this of all places to investigate this of all crimes? No one that *he* could think of.

"Right," called Hermione, lifting the needle from the turntable and cutting off the poet in full flight. " 'Webster was much possessed by death and saw the skull beneath the skin.' You too, by the look of you, so it's time for a gin."

"Maybe," said Bognor gloomily.

She arched eyebrows and neck simultaneously. "Too far gone even for the hair of the dog?"

"I'm not hung over. Someone hit me."

"I do know, as a matter of fact. Someone hit you, but you're hung over too. Or deserve to be. You stank of alcohol, but"—she raised a palm à la traffic policeman—"we are not going to start *that* all over again. You have suffered enough." She grinned. "Now I am going to change into something loose and easy and then you can tell me *all* about it. And while you're doing that, why don't you do something dangerous with gin. There are some madly exotic things in the kitchen: Cointreau, grenadine, passion fruit, Chinese gooseberries, even some packets of instant

Singapore Sling if you're feeling lazy." Saying which, she flounced off to what was presumably the bedroom.

Bognor, for his part, meandered into the kitchen, which had all the hallmarks of good living but not particularly good cooking: microwave oven, potted things, expensively canned things, bottled things from Fortnum's and Fauchon, Magimix. The smoked salmon in the fridge came from Ecclefechan. Bognor guessed that Dr. Frinton liked to eat out but prided herself on being able to rustle something up at a moment's notice without leaving her guest(s) alone for more than thirty seconds at a time. Slightly lugubriously he studied the drinks and finally opted for the Singapore Sling mix. His own gin, with a splash of Martini to judge from a quick sniff, he left alone and instead sloshed some fresh from the bottle into the blender, added almost a whole tray of ice, two sachets of crystals and some water, pressed the button and let it whoosh. It frothed into a pale pink, milkshake-like concoction which he guessed his hostess would have deftly decorated with slices of pineapple, sprigs of poinsettia and any other vegetation at hand. He, characteristically, poured it into two large tumblers, spilling a little, which he mopped up half-heartedly with a pocket handkerchief (being unable to locate the kitchen towels). When he had done he returned to the drawing room (salon, he thought, was probably a more appropriate word), glass in each hand, to find Hermione putting the final adjustment to jangling drop ear-rings which looked suspiciously like diamonds. She was wearing an extremely low-cut, white silk, quasi-diaphanous garment with sequins or some such all over it. These were silver and sparkled. She smelt overpoweringly of scent, which Bognor sensed was amazingly expensive. Inwardly he sighed. He wished he felt more in the mood for her.

"Ah," she said, eyeing the pink froth, "you cheated."

"'Fraid so," he admitted. "Not much of a bartender. Scotch and soda's about my limit."

"Consumption rather than construction?"

"You could put it like that."

She smiled and took one of the glasses. "Well, chin-chin," she said.

"Yes," said Bognor. "Chin-chin." He raised his glass and drank. It tasted very sweet and fruity. If he hadn't known, he would have assumed it was free of alcohol.

"I was beginning to think you'd never make it," she said. "Come and sit down and tell me all about it." She sank, in a seductively flowing movement, onto the sofa and patted the cushions in an invitation to Bognor to join her. He did, sitting primly and uncomfortably and well away from her. After contemplating him speculatively for a second, she put her feet up so that they rested on his lap, then she lay back and said, "If you're feeling particularly generous you may tickle my feet."

"Right," said Bognor.

"Oh, and could you be an angel and light me a cigarette? In the box there." She nodded towards a japanned papier-mâché object which Bognor opened to find full of Black Russians. He lit one and passed it to her. Accepting it, she allowed her hand to linger on his, and when she smiled a husky thank-you she looked him searchingly in the eyes, the sexual message unmistakable. Bognor looked away and sat more stiffly than ever.

"I just can't think who can have done it," he said.

"What, darling?" She exhaled very slowly, forming her lips in a tiny perfect "o."

"Attacked me."

"Oh, that."

"Yes, *that*. 'That,' as you put it, was exceedingly painful. I've had to have stitches."

"How many?"

"Three, actually."

She laughed. "I don't call that very many."

"It's quite enough," he said. "Why do you imagine it happened?"

"What do you want to know? *Who* dunnit? Or, *why* they dunnit?"

"If we know the second, we know the first."

Bognor was beginning to be muddled.

"First of all," she said, "someone broke into the Master's Lodgings to steal the confidential files. Particularly the ones for your year."

"Yes."

"Which they did."

"Yes."

"Then, when you return to your hotel room it is being done over, except you're too drunk to notice."

"I . . ."

She silenced him with a tap of her heel to the groin. "I thought you were going to tickle my feet."

"Oh."

"What's the matter? Don't my feet turn you on? Some men think my feet are my sexiest feature."

"Sorry, I'm not really into feet."

"Tell me what you *are* into then?" She stubbed out her cigarette and gave him a louchely come-hither smile.

"Nothing much at the moment," conceded Bognor, "except for solving these bloody murders."

"Well, it wasn't me."

"Could have been," said Bognor, "You had that hideous velocipede of yours. I was on foot."

"Velocette, darling. But why should I want to hit you on the head?"

"I don't know. You were being extremely disagreeable."

"You should see me when I try. When I'm really disagreeable I'm perfectly bloody."

"I can imagine."

She sipped at her drink and looked at him over the rim of the glass. "All right," she said, "we'll solve the murder and then relax. I can see you aren't going to be the slightest use until you've found out who did it. For my first thesis I wish to propose that despite any evidence to the contrary the murder of Beckenham and the murder of Vole have nothing whatever to do with each other."

"That's ridiculous."

"No more ridiculous than what's happened already. The Master revealed as a Soviet agent, found murdered. An Apocrypha alumnus shot dead by the Regius Professor of Sociology's hit man. The Regius Professor turns out to be Philby with knobs on. Beats *Dallas* any day of the week."

"And there's the small matter of the prospective Conservative Candidate for Sheen Central cheating in his final exams."

"I don't think we ought to get involved in all that again."

Bognor sighed. "Maybe not," he said. "I take your point. At the moment, the place is coming apart at the seams and anything's possible. So let's suppose you're right and the two murders have nothing to do with each other. What then?"

"Then we can eliminate Aveline and Vole as suspects for the Master's murder."

"Aveline was never a suspect for the Master's murder anyway."

"*I* suspected him." Hermione looked arch. She had finished her drink. "Shall we have another?" she asked.

Bognor said he wasn't particularly thirsty. She told him not to be silly. Together they went to the kitchen.

"Are you hungry?" she asked him.

"I'm always hungry," said Bognor, which was more or less true, though it was barely an hour since his toast and tea.

"I didn't have lunch," said Hermione. "What would you say to scrambled eggs with smoked salmon?"

"Yummy," said Bognor.

"And I tell you what, there's a bottle of Veuve Clicquot I keep in the fridge for emergencies such as this. While I'm scrambling, you open that. It should clear your head. And it's better for you than gin sling."

Bognor did as he was told. He hadn't the energy to do otherwise, though for once in his life he would just as soon have had cocoa.

"Do you think it could have been Edgware or Crutwell?" he asked as he tried to ease the cork out without hurting anyone.

"Why Edgware or Crutwell?"

"I saw them in the High that afternoon when I was out walking with Vole. At least, I think I did. They were in a bright-red Range Rover. I waved at them. Funny thing was that they didn't wave back. Didn't even acknowledge me. What do you make of that?"

Hermione whisked eggs and looked pensive. "You sure it was them?"

" 'Course I'm sure."

"Mmm."

Bognor managed to remove the cork with a gratifyingly discreet mini-burp and poured two glasses. Hermione took a sip and went on scrambling.

"So," she said, "Crutwell and Edgware were in Oxford that afternoon not wanting to be noticed. And had the bad luck to run into you. But why on earth should they go to your room at the Randolph? And what were they looking for?"

"Search me," he said.

Hermione cut off a large slab of butter and dropped it in the saucepan, then began to chop smoked salmon.

"Suppose," she said, "they think you've got something they want. Now what could that be?"

"Nothing. They have everything. The world is at their feet. Life is their oyster. Or words to that effect. I, I who have nothing . . . No, out of the question."

"No, no. Try to be literal." She added the smoked salmon and stirred. "They must have thought you had something that they were desperately keen to get hold of. What more likely than the Master's confidential files?"

"Because they contain the secrets of their guilty past, you mean?"

"Yes. Why not?" She snapped off the gas and spooned the eggs and fish onto two plates.

"Eggs Roseberry," said Bognor.

"Because of their racing colours."

"Something like that. But what . . ." Bognor took a plate and a glass and wandered back into the drawing room. "I mean, those two couldn't conceivably have guilty secrets. They were the great goody-goodies of the year. You could understand Rook or Vole or even me having something incriminating in our cupboards. But not Crutwell and Edgware."

"But if they had, they'd want the files. Both of them up for big jobs, remember. Both relying on the Master's references. With the Master's death, the files go public. Even if he was going to be nice about them while he was alive, he couldn't continue the cover-up once he was dead. Now just let's assume that they tried to steal the files from the Master's study but found someone had got there before them. Quite a chance they'd think that someone was you."

Bognor swallowed food. It was delicious. The Clicquot too. He unbent slightly. Hermione no longer had her feet on his lap but was herself sitting upright at the other end of the sofa, which was long. She could, he thought appreciatively, certainly scramble egg and she *was* jolly attractive. Nevertheless . . . He made himself think of Monica. Poor old Monica all on her own at home, opening a can of baked beans for her supper. Or, maybe, someone would ask her out. Anyway, he was far too unwell for sexual dalliance and, besides, there was work to be done.

"That's solved that, then." Bognor spoke almost flippantly. "Edgware and Crutwell were searching for the files in my room. Heard me coming, panicked, and hit me on the head. Bastards." Bognor said it with feeling. He still hurt like hell.

They went on eating in silence. Then Bognor said, "But I can't believe they killed the Master. Perhaps it was Vole."

"Or suicide." Hermione Frinton swallowed the last of her eggs and put her plate down on the low table.

"Mighty funny way to commit suicide," said Bognor. He too put his plate down and leaned back, feeling more relaxed than he had for ages. He closed his eyes and sighed, then opened them in a panic to find that he was looking straight into Dr. Frinton's at a range of inches.

Seconds later he was being kissed. At first he made absolutely no response, but as the kiss wore on he found that it was impossible not to be impressed and flattered by Dr. Frinton's ardour, enthusiasm and vigour. It seemed churlish for him not to kiss back. Also, after a while, his pride came into it. He was damned if he was going to be outkissed by a mere English tutor, even if she was a woman. The whole exercise was so exciting that after a while breathing became quite difficult, and every time he attempted to break away for air Hermione clamped her mouth even more tightly over his. He was afraid she'd break a tooth. She was also beginning to do arousing things with the rest of her body. Bells started to ring. For a while Bognor assumed the bells were in his mind, but after a while they sounded so real that he wondered if they came from outside it. Evidently he was not the only one to wonder about this because the doctor's ardour slowly diminished until she stopped kissing altogether and withdrew. She still had him pinioned securely to the sofa, but she stopped moving and lay panting lightly and listening to the insistent rings of the doorbell.

"Sugar!" she said, and attacked him again as passionately as before. The bell continued, so that she withdrew again after only about thirty seconds.

"Hadn't you better answer it?" asked Bognor, wondering if she had drawn blood. His lips felt as if they had been attacked by a ferret.

"They may go away," she said.

For a few seconds they went on listening. Again and again the bell rang. It became obvious that the caller was not going to leave. There was a pause, then shouting, muffled.

"Bloody hell!" said Hermione. She got up and went to the intercom switch, which she flicked on. Instantly the sound of an angry Chief Inspector Chappie filled the room. "I know you're there. Open up. No use taking the phone off the hook. It's important! Come on! Be your age." Hermione turned the machine off and gazed at Bognor, anguished. Bognor gazed back.

"He's not going to go away," said Bognor. "In fact, I'd say he was going to break the door down in a minute."

"Sod!" she said, brushing hair out of her eyes. "What a sense of timing!"

"Business before pleasure." Bognor smiled. He felt like Sir George White at the relief of Ladysmith. He smiled back at Hermione as she stood looking down at him, a passionate study in frustration. Eventually she went back to the machine, switched it on and called down to Smith. "Come on up," she said shortly. "Door's open." Bognor dabbed at his lips and straightened his tie. Hermione shrugged. "Can't win 'em all," she said. "I just hope there's a next time." Bognor was not sure what he thought about this, though he feared he might well succumb to temptation, enjoy himself hugely and then suffer fearful self-recrimination. Such reflections were interrupted by the irruption from the nether regions of the house of the Inspector himself, quivering with fury and self-importance. He took in the dishevelled appearance of his two colleagues plus the bottle of champagne and the empty plates, grinned sourly and said he was sorry to disturb them after hours, but one or two things had come up which he wanted discussed. He had tried phoning but the phone appeared to be off the hook.

"Correct," confirmed Hermione. "I always take the

phone off when I'm meditating. I must have forgotten to replace it. Simon came in mid-think."

Smith said nothing, but managed, with the tiniest flick of an eyebrow, to convey that gross impropriety had taken place.

"Drink?" asked Hermione, with the poise of the natural hostess. She gestured towards the half-empty bottle of Clicquot.

"Got anything a bit less arty-tarty?"

"Scotch?"

"Scotch would be perfect."

Hermione went to fetch some. Smith turned to Bognor. "You seem to have made a speedy recovery," he said sardonically. "Wouldn't have thought of you as being a particularly fast worker. Congratulations."

"As a matter of fact . . ." Bognor began, but was silenced by his hostess' return.

Smith accepted his drink, which looked stiff, took a sip and said, "Right, then. Some new facts have come to light. First off, one of my men found a briefcase at the Old Bakehouse, initials 'S.V.' for Sebastian Vole, sundry papers of no interest or importance but an empty folder clearly indicating that it once contained the missing file from the Master's study."

"Gosh!" said Bognor. "So it was Vole who nicked them."

"Vole nicked 'em and Aveline now has 'em." The Inspector licked his lips. "A nice little bonus for the Ivans as the Cold War enters its next round."

"Except that if Beckenham was one of theirs," said Hermione, "they'd know already."

"Wouldn't be sure of that," said the Inspector. "Can't say I begin to understand where the loyalties of that sort of person lie, but I'm inclined to think that there are people who put College before God, Queen or Country."

"Very perceptive," said Bognor. "You mean Beckenham

would have betrayed anything to the Russians except the good name of the college."

"That's exactly what I mean," said Smith. He looked at Bognor quizzically. "You extracting the Michael?" he asked suspiciously.

"Not in the least," said Bognor. "I think there's much truth in what you say. But if Vole stole the files, where does that get us?"

"Can't say for sure," said the Inspector. "That's one of the things I want to discuss. Now, another thing is your Humphrey Rook's got alibis all over the auction. Seems to have spent all relevant periods closeted with impeccable witnesses in the City of London. That doesn't mean he's innocent of the Master's murder, but it does mean he didn't break into the Randolph and clobber you."

"I see." Bognor poured more Clicquot for himself and Hermione.

"However"—the Inspector stabbed the air with a stubby forefinger, indicating that significant revelation was about to ensue—"two of our candidates are missing."

"Missing?" said Hermione. "This business of people missing isn't good enough. Who now, apart from Aveline?"

"Ian Edgware and Peter Crutwell," said Smith, eyes gleaming.

"And what do you mean 'missing'?" asked Bognor. "I saw them yesterday in a red Range Rover in the High. We were talking about it just before you arrived."

The Inspector let this blatant piece of delusion pass without comment. Instead, he said, "I called the FO and they said Edgware was on leave. When I called home his wife said he was on a special Foreign Office course."

"Learning Urdu and Unarmed Combat, no doubt," said Bognor flippantly.

"*And*," continued Smith, "when I got on to Ampleside I was told that Crutwell was away on a recce in the Western

Highlands of Scotland. Something to do with the school commando camp next winter. Or the Duke of Edinburgh's Award Scheme."

"The Duke of Edinburgh has a lot to answer for," said Bognor with feeling. "I suppose Crutwell is sleeping rough and living off the land miles from the nearest telephone. That would be in character."

"That's what they told me."

"And when's he due back?"

"They don't seem to know."

"Honestly," said Bognor, "it costs £4,000 a year to send a child to Ampleside and they haven't the foggiest idea where their staff are. If I were a Ampleside parent I'd be hopping. Absolutely hopping!"

"Oh, God"—Hermione stifled a mock yawn—"this is getting us nowhere. In fact"—and she shot both men meaningful glances—"I've been getting nowhere all day."

Bognor was about to expostulate, but Smith spoke first.

"I'm not at all happy with the way our investigations are proceeding," he said. "We started off with what could perfectly well have been passed off as a heart attack and now we've got two murders and a major political scandal. We've got a handful of suspects who are turning out to have some surprisingly dubious sides to their characters, but we're no further on than when we started."

"Less," said Bognor, unnecessarily, "minus two, plus nothing."

"So what do you suggest, super-sleuths?" asked Hermione.

"Wish I knew." The Inspector looked at the end of his tether. He might not have been hit on the head, but he had been up all night and he was making a negative impression on the case. He was becoming depressed, and he was exhausted.

"Do we have anything more on the stuff in the bottle? The stuff that actually killed him."

Smith shook his head. "Not difficult to find if you know

a chemist. Our suspects would have been able to get hold of it. No problem."

"What about finding traces of it anywhere else? Have we searched?" Hermione looked almost as depressed as her guests.

"No sight nor sound," said Smith, "but I wouldn't expect it. We're dealing with educated murderers here, not your common or garden rapist or bank robber. This is intellectual stuff, and if my hunch is right, intellectuals make different sorts of mistakes to your ordinary villain."

"But we're dealing with amateurs," said Bognor.

"The Inspector's right," said Hermione. "Amateurs, perhaps, but educated amateurs. Apocrypha men with all the arrogance which that implies. Arrogant amateurs, my darlings, will make mistakes. Given time."

"Aveline wasn't an amateur," said Smith, with respect. "Proper pro that one."

Bognor yawned. "I don't know about you lot, but I'm just about ready for bed," he announced plaintively.

Hermione Frinton gave him a poisonous glare which made it abundantly clear that she had been ready for bed about an hour ago.

Bognor flushed. The Inspector inspected the highly polished toes of his functional black shoes.

"And so where precisely," enquired Hermione in glacial tones, "do we go from here?"

Bognor was on the point of saying "back to the Randolph" but quailed and thought better of it. "Seems to me," he said, "that you two should go over all the Oxford evidence. Such as it is. I'd better check in with Parkinson, who's been trying to get hold of me all day. And then I shall submit Master Rook to a rigorous interrogation on the subject of his political theory paper. And allied matters."

A certain glumness greeted this less-than-sensational proposal.

"All right," he said, "anyone got any better ideas?"

The silence implied that no one had. Smith said he had better be getting home. He would do his best to track down Edgware and Crutwell. Hermione would go over the events of the evening with Mitten once more. All three knew that they had little better to offer than a collective Micawber. At present and until something turned up (which, they might say, they were hourly expecting), they had nothing to do but go through motions. In case of anything turning up (of which they were far from confident), they would go about their duties with renewed enthusiasm. But for the moment they were grave, not to say miserable.

Smith offered Bognor a lift and Bognor accepted. Lingering on the threshold as the Inspector descended the stairs, Bognor kissed Dr. Frinton chastely.

"Are you *sure* you won't stay?" she asked, running a finger down his stubbly cheek.

"I'd love to," he said very quietly, "but I'd be quite useless. I'm absolutely knackered. Simply couldn't cope."

She shrugged, uncharacteristically subdued. "Story of my life," she said, "luck of the Frintons."

"Anyway, I'm a happily married man. You shouldn't make passes at married men."

"Don't be absurd," she purred, a little humour coming back into her voice, "I *only* make passes at happily married men. Single men are *deathly* dull and I'm incorrigible. I shan't give up, you know."

From down below in the area of the house reserved for the International Vegan Brotherhood for International Peace and Harmony the voice of the Chief Inspector Chappie came echoing up, sepulchral yet sardonic.

"Knock it off, you two," it said. Remember, I'm an old friend of Mrs. Bognor. You've had enough trouble for one day, Bognor."

With heavy heart and head, Bognor had to acknowledge that this was true. Slowly, he turned and went down the stairs, virtue intact, *joie de vivre* diminished, mission unfulfilled.

CHAPTER 7

Bognor was allergic to banks. They made his palms sweat. Even when he presented a cheque for a fiver he expected the cashier to refuse to cash it. He regarded his bank manager, a perfectly amiable Rotarian and scratch golfer, with the same apprehension as his dentist. He didn't understand money. He never had any. Yet it controlled his life and therefore, by logical extension, bankers were to be feared. They controlled his money supply which, in a materialist society, was the staff of life. Try as he might, he could not like anyone who wielded such authority over him, any more than he could bring himself to, really, like Parkinson.

These thoughts passed through his mind as he sat, sweating and twitching, in the antiseptic grandeur of the reception area at Lowthers. Lowthers was a merchant bank. There was a difference, Bognor realised, between the merchant bank and the high street bank, but as far as he was concerned it was all money, and therefore to be treated with caution and distrust. Lowthers was a grand old bank in the Rothschild mould. The original Lowther had financed the Cabots' trips to Newfoundland almost five hundred years ago, and Lowthers had been juggling money ever since. Lowthers, he had been told, had at least a dozen African and South American governments in their pockets. Not nice ones, either. Lowthers had never been strong on scruple. A few years ago they had sold their old Victorian premises in Leadenhall Street, very close to their deadly rivals, Barings, and moved into this glass-and-concrete monster in London Wall.

Bognor, arriving dead on time for his hastily arranged meeting with Humphrey Rook, had been given a cup of coffee and told to wait. In the nicest possible way by the nicest possible twin set and pearl receptionist. Nicest possible coffee too, out of the nicest possible china. He sighed and stopped pretending to read the pink pages of the *Financial Times*. The reproduction panelling of the reception area was lined with Lowthers. The artists who had painted them were no more than passing competent, but they had captured the defining family characteristic, which seemed to Bognor to be greed.

It had not been a good morning. Bognor was not at his best, and he had had to catch an early train. Parkinson, he was bound to say, had been less than cordial.

"Having a crack at starting World War Three single-handed, I hear" had been his opening words. Bognor had not had the energy or even the inclination to defend himself from his superior's attacks. Instead, he sat sullenly waiting for Parkinson to finish and let him get on with his job. Parkinson, he reflected as he gazed down the line of portraits opposite him, had Lowther eyes: small and mean. There was no generosity in those eyes, no love, no compassion. They were not life-enhancing eyes. Bognor's eyes, though increasingly bloodshot and never especially wide open, had, he liked to think, a warmth about them. They were indicators of an open personality. Women responded to them. Parkinson's eyes were like animated marbles. His mouth wasn't up to much, either. He completely failed to understand the complexities and difficulties with which Bognor was constantly assailed. It was all very well warming a revolving civil service chair under that institutional portrait of the Queen. Naturally life looked pretty straightforward from that side of the desk with an index-linked pension and membership of the Reform Club claimed on expenses. All Bognor got was luncheon vouchers. No doubt about it, he was simply not appreciated. It was men like him who made Britain Great while the bosses, people like Parkinson and the Lowthers, got all the credit and all the loot.

"Mr. Rook will see you now, Mr. Bognor." The receptionist spoke loudly and frostily, causing Bognor to suppose that she was saying the sentence for the second time.

"Good," said Bognor, getting to his feet and dusting his trousers, which had become flecked with biscuit crumbs.

"Take the lift to the seventeenth, and Mr. Rook's secretary will meet you."

"Thanks." Bognor gave what was intended to be a haughty smile. He wanted to convey the impression that he was here to negotiate the multi-million-pound financing of some ritzy petro-chemical plant and was not accustomed to being kept waiting. Alas, it was all too obvious that he was perfectly used to being kept waiting. Never mind, murder was more interesting than petro-chemicals. If the girl behind the desk knew that he was interviewing Rook about murder, surely she would have been impressed. No. Bognor pursed his lips glumly. Probably not.

Alighting at the seventeenth, he was greeted by another aloofly polite and immaculate secretary of the type that, on first and all subsequent impressions, confers status on the boss. It was quite clear from this girl's elegance, grooming, and demeanour that Rook was earning comfortably in excess of £25,000 a year and had the key to whatever washroom or other part of the building was at the top of the executive tree at Lowthers. Hardly surprising. Apart from being such a smooth operator, Rook had married a Lowther. At least, Bognor thought he'd married a Lowther. He'd lay long odds he had at least one steady mistress by now. Such was life.

"Simon!" exclaimed Rook unctuously, oiling out from behind a behemoth of a desk and advancing on his old Apocryphal friend with a disingenuous beam and an outstretched hand. "I *am* sorry to have kept you. Something cropped up at the last moment. In fact, between you and me, Mangolo was going bankrupt and we've just had to bail her out."

They shook hands and Rook returned to the safety of his revolving armchair.

"Mangolo?" said Bognor. "I knew the Umdaka once."

"George," said Rook. "Charming fellow. Not an enormous amount between the ears, and given to extravagance. Hence his country's bankruptcy. Never mind, what's a few billion between friends? Coffee?"

"Thanks. I've just had some."

"Ah," said Rook, "good. Good. Well now . . ." He placed the tips of his fingers together and smiled. "What can I do for you?"

Behind him loomed St. Paul's Cathedral, miraculously close. Bognor pondered the proximity of God and Mammon and wondered if Rook was given to ostentatious little excursions to midweek communions. He wouldn't put it past him.

"This murder business," said Bognor. "It's about that."

Rook made a long lugubrious face, indicating concern and gravitas. "Yes," he said. "I imagined it was about that. Wretched business. Naturally, anything I can do to help. Anything at all."

"There's been another, I'm afraid."

"Another?"

"Yes. Vole."

Rook seemed genuinely surprised. "Vole?!" he said. "You mean Seb Vole? Murdered? Whatever for? I mean, who in their right mind would want to do in a chap like Seb Vole?"

"We're almost certain it was Aveline," said Bognor, "but until we are absolutely certain I'd rather you didn't say anything about all this. It is rather confidential, so I'd be obliged if you'd keep it under your hat."

"Rather," said Rook, eyes wide. "But why Aveline? You do mean Aveline. Macho Max? The Regius?"

"Absolutely," said Bognor, lowering his voice the greater to impress the banker. He was disagreeably aware that impressing Rook was important to him. Silly, but there it was.

"But why?"

Bognor's voice dropped another few decibels, so that it was only just the loud side of audible.

"This really is extremely hush-hush," he whispered. "It turns out that Aveline was some sort of Blunt figure, only dangerous. Really significant. The difference between being able to tell the Russians about Poussin and being able to tell them about . . . well, you know Aveline."

"I thought I did," said Rook. He smoothed back his already smooth sparse hair. "But I never . . ."

"No," conceded Bognor, "nor me. Anyway, to cut a long story short, poor old Vole rumbled him. He was researching a magnum opus on moles, fifth-columnists, quislings and their ilk. When he confronted Aveline with this, Aveline had him shot."

"Good grief!" Rook *was* impressed. "And where does Beckenham's murder fit in with this? You mean to say Aveline had him killed too."

"I'm afraid I can't divulge that," said Bognor. "Our enquiries are still at a somewhat delicate stage."

"But good heavens, man, it's obvious. If Aveline was going round bumping people off, then he obviously did in the Master."

Bognor smiled tolerantly. "I'm afraid detection's a rather more complicated and sophisticated business than that," he said. "No use flying by the seat of your pants in our line of country." He was sure this was the sort of language Rook used when dealing with clients. "The fact is," he continued, "we have to be alive to the possibility that the two killings were entirely—I emphasise *entirely*—unconnected."

"Oh, really!" said Rook. "That's simply not on. College rumbles along for hundreds of years with nothing more dramatic than the occasional rustication or some idiot hurting himself climbing in late at night, then all of a sudden there's a double murder and you say it's pure coincidence."

"It may look peculiar, but life often does."

Rook looked utterly incredulous.

"The fact is that we have reason to suppose that the Master may have been killed for his files."

"For his files?"

"Or, more accurately, for the suppression of what was in those files."

"Oh, yes," said Rook slowly. "Such as?"

"We recently discovered that the Master's study had been broken into and our year's files stolen."

"Nothing to do with me," said Rook evenly. "I was here all the time."

"How do you know what time I'm talking about?"

"Because I had a frankly rather impertinent call from someone called Smith. A policeman."

"Yes," said Bognor, "of course. Nevertheless, I put it to you that there was material in those files which you would very much prefer to be suppressed. Particularly"—and here he injected a definite note of menace into his voice—"in view of your involvement with the vacancy at Sheen Central."

"What are you talking about?"

"I think you know very well what I'm talking about." Bognor felt he should be enjoying himself more. By rights, he should have the upper hand. Rook should be squirming by now. Putty in his hands. Ready to confess to anything. Instead, he seemed surprisingly chipper, and it was Bognor who was becoming unnerved.

"Haven't a clue, old man," said Rook. He sat back, waiting, evidently, for enlightenment.

"A little matter of your final examination papers. Political theory, to be precise. The fact that you owed your first to the pure alpha you got in political theory and that you would never have done it if you hadn't snaffled a look at the draft paper in the Master's study weeks before the exam took place."

"Oh," said Rook. He smiled indulgently. "That!"

"Yes," said Bognor. "That."

"Well?"

"What do you mean 'well'?" Bognor was becoming distinctly panicky now. That was not at all how he had imagined the meeting. "That's cheating," he blustered. "I can't think the electors of Sheen Central would be any too happy to think they were being represented by a cheat and a liar."

"I don't see why not," said Rook. He smiled. "No, seriously, old man, tell me exactly what it is that you're getting at. Are you implying that I killed Beckenham?"

"Um," said Bognor, "well, in a manner of speaking. That is to say . . . yes."

"But you don't really believe it, do you?"

"Shouldn't I?"

"I know you're not exactly alpha material," said Rook, "but you're not a *complete* fool."

Bognor said nothing.

"I suppose Molly told you," continued Rook. "You knew her on the *Globe* when you were dealing with that St. John Derby scandal, didn't you? It's true it's not something I choose to broadcast to all and sundry. But it's a long time ago and even if old Beckenham had chosen to blurt it out to the selection committee at Sheen, which I very much doubt, I can't see it would do me any harm."

"But it was cheating."

"Now look, old fruit. Put yourself in my position. I have a tutorial with our much-loved Master. Right? Are you following me?"

"Yes."

"So I turn up at his study as per normal and I find he's not there. Slipped out for a slash. Right. Still with me?"

Bognor nodded. "So I'm standing there killing time and

what do I see lying about for all to see but a Political Theory paper. And since Political Theory is what the Master and I meet to discuss every week, what could be more natural than that I should take a bit of a gander at it, eh?"

Bognor nodded. "Go on," he said forlornly. Rook was going to make an excellent Member of Parliament. He had the successful politician's knack of making rank dishonesty seem perfectly honourable. In a second, he would be making it seem courageous, too.

"As it happens, I'd read half the questions before I realised it was our own paper and not an old one. By which time the damage was done. I didn't try to hide it either. The Master *knew* . . . If anyone was to blame, it was him. He could have produced a new paper."

Bognor gazed glumly over Rook's shoulder at Sir Christopher Wren's masterpiece. The trouble with Rook, or one of the troubles with Rook, was his plausibility. Impossible to know whether he was telling the truth or not. But his defence did have an awful conviction.

"Do you know if the Sheen selection committee asked the Master for a reference?"

"As it happens, yes. For the very good reason that I gave his name as a referee. What's more, I heard from him a couple of days before the Gaudy, congratulating me on making the short list and saying that if his testimonial had anything to do with it I'd win the nomination nem. con. And if you don't believe me, I've got the letter at home. I imagine Beckenham would have kept a copy of the testimonial on file, too. So, one way and another, I rather think I'm in the clear."

"Yes," said Bognor wearily, "it does look like it."

"Sorry about that."

"What?"

"Foiling you. I do see that you want to make an arrest." Rook stood up and paced to a bookcase covered with photographs of Lowthers, children, dogs and one or two pictures of Rook shaking hands with assorted Tory notables, including Mrs. Thatcher. As he paced, he jangled the change in his trouser pocket in a manner which Bognor found profoundly irritating.

"Nothing personal," said Bognor, lying.

"Oh, quite," said Rook, not believing him but having already thought of a satisfactory way of levelling the score. "But"—he paused and rubbed his jaw thoughtfully—"I think I may be able to help you out, old boy. You see, there's something I dare say you don't know and which might be disturbingly relevant. *Disturbingly* relevant, now I come to think of it." He sat down again, heavily, and Bognor was struck by the fleshiness which prosperous middle age was bringing to that once quite gaunt-boned face.

"I expect I'm right in thinking that your prime suspects are those of us who were having a noggin with the old bean after our less than sumptuous repast on Saturday evening."

"Just about."

"Mitten's men, in fact."

"Yes."

"Not Mitten, though? Or that Frinton piece with the legs?"

"I don't think . . ." said Bognor. "That is to say . . ."

"Do you want help or don't you?"

"Naturally I want any help you can give me, but I can't tell you everything about our enquiries. Besides," Bognor rallied, "if you did have helpful information and were to withhold it, then you'd be obstructing the police in the exercise of their duties."

"Would I?"

"Indubitably."

"Well, if you say so. It's scarcely relevant, since I'm going to help you anyway, whether you like it or not." He smiled, showing a wide expanse of gum and uneven teeth, not very white. "You were quite young when you came up, weren't you?"

"Not especially," said Bognor. "I didn't do National Service or anything like that, but then none of us did."

"I mean, young for your age. Led a sheltered sort of a life. Hadn't knocked around a great deal. Not entirely clear about what was what."

"You could say that, I suppose. It never really occurred to me."

"No. It wouldn't, would it?" It struck Bognor quite suddenly that Rook must have been the school bully before coming up to Oxford. "The point I'm making," said Rook, standing up again and jangling the change in his pocket more ferociously than ever, "is that you may have thought one or two people were nicer than they really were."

"I tend to think the best of people." Bognor was painfully aware of sounding prissy.

Rook gave him another gummy smile.

"Spot on, old fruit. I, on the other hand, temper my Christian humility and love of my fellow man with a certain realism. I do happen to believe in original sin."

Bognor hadn't the first idea of what he was driving at. However, he had a shrewd-enough idea of Rook's character to know that he was driving at something.

"Take Edgware and Crutwell," said Rook.

Bognor frowned and, metaphorically speaking, took a firm grasp on both.

"Pure as the driven snow, no doubt. Butter wouldn't melt in their mouths. Eh?"

"That's putting it a bit strong," said Bognor, "but I never heard anything said against them."

"Never heard about the Apocrypha Choir School racket?"

"No."

"That's what I mean, you see." Rook looked avuncular, like a schoolmaster imparting the facts of life to a confirmation candidate. "Well," he said, "I wouldn't tell you now except that the circumstances demand it. I make no accusations, mind. I'm simply pointing out that people other than me have more compelling reasons for wanting those files kept secret. Now tell me, do you remember that both Crutwell and Edgware sang in the chapel choir?"

"Yes. Peter Crutwell was a bass. Ian Edgware was a tenor."

"You never questioned it?"

"No."

Rook looked up at the ceiling as if to say that the naïvety of some people was truly staggering.

"Nothing to do with music. Nothing to do with Christianity," said Rook. "So what's left?"

"To judge from your expression and general manner, I assume you're going to say 'choirboys.'"

"'Fraid so. Edgware and Crutwell were the original 'Bertie Wooftahs,' but it wasn't just each other they were interested in. They were after the pretty little boys in the choir."

"Crutwell and Edgware? But they're both happily married with children. As a matter of fact, they both, quite independently, showed me photographs of their families the other night at the Gaudy."

"Well, there you are, then." Rook smiled his sardonic smile again. "That ought to have aroused your suspicions. Never trust anyone who shows you snaps of their kiddiwinks at dinner. Not natural."

Bognor glanced ostentatiously at the assorted family pictures along the top of the bookcase. Rook fielded the reference. "Hardly the same thing, old dear," he said, simpering, "but it's worse than that. You see, Crutwell and Edgware realised they were on to rather a good thing with the Apocrypha Choir School. Quite the sweetest little boys in town and they'd do anything for a packet of crisps or a box of smarties. Or so I'm told. So our friends turned it into a commercial operation."

"Oh, come on! Now you are pulling my leg." But even as he said it, Bognor realised that Rook was being quite serious.

"I'll bet it's all on the file," he said. "They were running a child prostitution racket. That's what it comes down to. But there was a scandal in the end. It was inevitable. They tried to be careful, but after a while someone talked. Funnily enough, I don't believe any parent ever discovered, so old Beckenham and the choirmaster managed to hush it up."

"How did *you* know?"

Rook smirked again. "They weren't all that clever at telling a wooftah from what it now pleases those who know to call 'a straight.' They decided I was a bit bent and offered me the star alto for a fiver. Not my taste, so I declined."

"And told the Master?"

"Not me," said Rook. "No reason to. I don't know how old Beckenham found out, but he kept his nose close to the ground. He missed less than you suppose."

"They never propositioned me," said Bognor, not sure whether to be proud or aggrieved.

"Naturally not. You were far too pea-green incorruptible. As I said, 'young for your age.' Besides, you were always entwined with that big goofy thing from St. Hilda's who played lacrosse."

"LMH, actually," said Bognor peevishly, "and netball, not lacrosse."

"Monica something."

"Monica Bognor, actually." Bognor knew when to be stuffy. "We got married."

"Did you?" Rook looked speculative. "Anyway, it was hardly surprising they didn't offer you choirboys when you were embroiled with a big girl like that."

"I see."

"What I'm getting at," said Rook, "is that it's one thing to have a wooftah Ambassador. They're two a penny. So it doesn't matter if Edgware likes a bit of the other, but it's scarcely going to appeal to the Governors of Fraffleigh. Frankly, Crutwell's lucky to have got as far as he has in education. Housebeak at Ampleside is not to be sneezed at, but I wouldn't be happy if I were a parent of one of his boys. It's not the undermatrons he's interested in, I can tell you. My guess is that Crutwell, who's always been an ambitious little shit, would do practically anything for a head-mastership."

"Kill?" asked Bognor.

"I'd have said he was too wet," opined Rook, "but you can never tell with wooftahs. We employ one or two here. Hard as nails, some of them. Bloody ruthless, I can tell you. But not Crutwell."

"As it happens, Crutwell is at this very moment bashing around the mountains of Western Scotland, sleeping rough and generally being phenomenally Spartan," said Bognor.

"Typical wooftah behaviour," said Rook. "Doesn't prove a blind thing except he's a masochist. Certainly doesn't mean he slipped a lethal dose of something in the Master's raspberry fire-water. And now"—he fished out a gold watch from his waistcoat, squinted at it and went on—"I'm afraid I'm going to have to shove you out. Henry Kissinger's lunching. Do hope I've been some help." He stood, jangled some change, shook hands, beamed automatically. "Tamsen will see you out," he said. "*Very* best of luck, and if there's anything else I can possibly do to help, don't hesitate to let me know. I'm often here."

Bognor was angry and miserable about this encounter but not nearly as angry as he was half-way through the afternoon, when, dozing at his desk, he received a phone call from Molly Mortimer of the *Globe*.

"Got you, you beast!" she shrilled. "You owe me information. You owe me a scoop."

"I can't give what I don't have," he muttered.

"Don't be absurd," said Molly. "You and I came to a little deal over dinner before that monstrous woman in leather dragged you away."

"Remind me."

"A quid pro quo. I told you Cousin Humphrey's hidden secret, and you were going to let me have the murderer, exclusive."

"Did I say that?" Bognor had genuinely forgotten the greater part of his Italian meal with Miss Mortimer, but now that she mentioned it, the alleged deal did have a gruesome familiarity.

"You most certainly did, and I hope you're not going to try and renege."

"I never renege," said Bognor. "Well, almost never. It's the family motto: 'Never renege.' "

"Don't be flippant with me, Simon ducky." Bognor frowned and tried to remember when anyone had last called him ducky. It sounded suspiciously as if Molly had been out to lunch. Still was out to lunch, come to that.

"So," she said, "are you going to tell me who did it? Or am I going to have to tell you?"

"Don't be silly," said Bognor with asperity. "I'm extremely busy. I'm extremely tired. I'm not at all well. I've had a distinctly tiresome meeting with your Cousin Humphrey. I'm still embroiled in a complicated and intractable murder investigation, and I'm not allowed to talk to the press. You'll have to go through the Press Office. Ask for someone called Witherspoon. Or Watherspoon. Something like that. He's your man."

"I'm not press, I'm Molly."

"Look, Molly, I don't want to seem brusque, but I am rather tied up at the moment. I'm in the middle of a meeting and I have someone coming to see me in ten minutes and . . ." None of this was even half true but Bognor was finding such evasions increasingly easy.

"What I'm trying to tell you Simon, dear, is that I know about Aveline."

Bognor stopped slouching and sat very upright, spine tingling, stomach churning, head throbbing, adrenaline pumping to every extremity.

"You what?" he said, trying to keep the concern out of his voice.

"I know that Max Aveline has disappeared and that he is wanted for the murder of Lord Beckenham and a man called Vole."

"Not true," said Bognor. "That is to say, 'no comment.'" Inwardly he was seething. That bloody man Rook. He should never have told him. He had only done it because he wanted to impress him. Vanity, vanity. Rook's arrogant, indolent superiority had trapped him into indiscretion. He would fix him, though Heaven alone knew how.

"I hate to say this, Simon"—suddenly Molly sounded quite sober—"but I've spoken to the editor and we're going to lead on it tomorrow. We've done some checking already. We've found that Max Aveline has vanished and we've found that this chap Vole's been killed and we've learned from Vole's publishers that he was working on some espionage project, and we've got our Whitehall correspondent burrowing away. So it seems perverse of you not to tell me what's going on. Otherwise, we may make mistakes. Wouldn't it be better for us to get it absolutely one hundred per cent right?

"I can't," he said tersely. "You know I can't. It's more than my life's worth. Your Cousin Humphrey's probably ruined me by doing this. And you won't be able to publish. We'll slap a 'D' notice on it."

"We shan't pay any attention."

"Then you and your editor will go to the Tower."

"Nobody worries about 'D' notices," snapped Molly. "We shall publish."

"And be damned," said Bognor and crashed down the receiver. For several moments he stayed looking at the telephone, wondering if there was any point in ringing her back and being apologetic and conciliatory. None, he decided. Molly was doing her job. You couldn't blame her for it. She was a good journalist, according to her lights, and one of a good journalist's lights was knowing how and when to betray your friends. Bognor was realist enough to know that a trustworthy journalist wasn't doing his job properly. But what to do?

On mature consideration and with very great reluctance indeed, he acknowledged that the only course open to him was to confide in his boss. Accordingly he padded along to his office and barged in gratified to discover him drinking tea and pondering the *Times* Crossword. He looked abashed.

"You're supposed to knock, Bognor," he said, trying to win back some initiative.

"Sorry," said Bognor, "I forgot. We've run into a bit of a flap."

"Oh, yes?" Parkinson regarded him steadily and expressionlessly. "Bit of a flap, eh? Someone else shuffled off the coil as the result of your incompetence?"

"No. Nothing like that."

"Good. Good. I'm delighted to hear it."

"I'm afraid the press have got hold of the Aveline story."

Parkinson picked up his pencil and bit into it.

"Got hold of the Aveline story," he repeated.

"I'm rather afraid so, yes."

"Held a press conference, did you? Or merely put out a release to the PA?"

"There appears to have been some sort of leak," said Bognor, ignoring this irritatingly heavy sarcasm, "from the Oxford end."

"A leak from the Oxford end. I see." Parkinson was at his most withering. "No point in thinking it's anything to do with a sieve like you?"

Bognor flinched but said nothing.

"How do you know this?"

"I was telephoned by a reporter on the *Globe*."

"Of course. You have these unfortunate associations

with the *Globe*. You are aware that it is an offence to talk
to the press. That's Witherspoon's job."

"That's what I told them."

Parkinson glared. "Don't get clever with me, Bognor,"
he said.

"I wasn't being clever. Absolutely not."

"No. Silly of me."

Parkinson shut his eyes and appeared to be muttering
something silently but ferociously.

"You all right?" asked Bognor.

"No," said Parkinson, opening his eyes again. "I am not
in the least all right and I am, as they say, all the worse for
seeing you. I would be obliged if you would remove yourself forthwith. If I were you, I should hide under the larg-
est stone you can find. Meanwhile, I shall endeavour to sal-
vage something from the wreckage." He shut his eyes.
"Please go!" he hissed. "At once. And stay away."

Bognor, for once, did as he was told.

Back in his office, he discovered that Inspector Smith had
telephoned and left a message. The girl on the switch-
board who had taken it said succinctly, "A Mr. Smith rang
and said that a Mr. Crutwell was back at home now and
Mr. Edgware with him."

"That all?" he asked.

"Yes," said the girl. "He seemed to think you'd understand."

Bognor sighed. No point in hanging around the office
and possibly being seen by Parkinson. It was a good excuse
for getting away. He had little hope of a meeting with the
two men yielding anything of interest. In view of Rook's
appalling treachery, he was disinclined to believe his story
of the Apocrypha Choir School racket, which was almost
certainly a malicious red herring designed to create bad
blood between Bognor and Crutwell and Edgware and
deflect attention from Rook. Nevertheless, it would have
to be checked, unpalatable though the checking would un-

doubtedly be. He wondered whether to arrange an appointment or simply turn up, whether to drive or go by train. Decisions, decisions, he thought desperately and decided to toss a coin. His mind was not up to freedom of choice. As the result of this, he set off by train, unannounced.

Ampleside was not a major public school, and yet to call it a minor public school was less than fair. It hovered in a sort of no-man's-land between the excellent and the mediocre, never quite sure whether it was on the verge of promotion from the second division or relegation from the first. If you accepted Waugh's Grades (Leading School, First-rate School, Good School and School), then Ampleside was either among the last of the Leading or the First of the First-rate. But Waugh's caveat about these definitions should be remembered: "Frankly," said Mr. Levy, "school is pretty bad." Ampleside was not bad, not bad at all, but it seldom attained excellence or even aspired to it. It was worthy, it was hard-working, it was hearty and it was dull.

Reaching Ampleside Station shortly after six, Bognor, who had never previously visited the place, learned that the school and its constituent houses were on the outskirts of town, some fifteen minutes' walk away. It was a fine evening and, despite the continuing fragility of his condition, Bognor had no objection to hoofing it. The exercise might clear the brain. In any case, walking was the next best thing to jogging. If he walked often and fast enough, he might one day build up to a gentle job. It was unlikely but possible.

The town was quiet, pleasant without being picturesque and just too small to be disfigured by an excrescence of large chain stores and supermarkets. In the wide main street with a number of battered half-timbered houses Bognor noticed a couple of almost serious bookshops and one or two pubs which looked like serious drinking places. He was tempted to drop in for a pint but thought better of it.

Time for that on his return, always provided he was successful.

The school itself was less attractive than the town, being a Victorian foundation with twentieth-century additions. This meant an imposing bogus baronial front with a high tower over a gateway which was a weak parody of Apocrypha Great Gate. Also glass-and-concrete science blocks. It had space, however, much of it green and well mown and peopled in places with boys in white playing out the last overs of the afternoon's cricket. Under the arch was a porter's lodge, and here Bognor stopped to enquire as to the whereabouts of Mr. Crutwell.

"Who?" asked the school custos, a scarlet-faced pensioner of vaguely military mien.

"Crutwell," said Bognor, "Mr. Crutwell. He's a housemaster."

The custos shook his head in evident perplexity. "Who do you say?" he asked again.

Bognor felt the panic rising like sap. It was Ampleside that Crutwell taught at, surely? Or had he misheard or misunderstood? Could it have been Ardingly or Alleyns or Allhallows or Abingdon or Aldenham or even Ample*forth?*

"Crutwell," he said again, "Mr. Crutwell. C-R-U-T-W-E-L-L. Crutwell."

The custos stared as blankly as before and then suddenly his face became suffused with understanding.

"You mean Mr. Crutwell," he said, smiling broadly at Bognor as if *he* was the fool.

Bognor was on the point of expostulating but realised it would only complicate matters. "Crutwell," he said, smiling, "That's the chap."

"He's Housemaster of Bassingthwaite," said the custos.

"Is he? And where's that?"

The porter grumbled to his feet, holding his back like a rheumatic in a Will Hay comedy, and staggered out into the evening's shadows. Much pointing, gesticulating and unintelligible direction-finding ensued.

"Fine," said Bognor. "Thanks very much. I'm sure I'll find it quite all right." He set off into the sunset, blinking slightly and resolved to ask the first sane boy he saw where Bassingthwaite really was. From behind came a shout. It was the custos. Swearing silently, Bognor retraced his steps.

"You looking for Mr. Crutwell?"

"That was the general sort of idea, yes."

"You won't find him at Bassingthwaite."

"Oh. Just as well you caught me. I might have had a wasted journey. Where will he be?"

"At Big Field watching Potters."

"Of course," said Bognor. "Silly of me. I should have known. Big Field, watching Potters. Right, then. I suppose that's Potters over there?" He pointed towards the grandest of the cricket pitches, the only one with spectators.

The custos nodded.

"Well, thank you so much. I'm much indebted to you." And once more Bognor strode off past the ivy-covered red brick, through the lengthening shadows, across a gravelled quadrangle, through a post-war cloister complete with war memorial to Ampleside's glorious dead, and out onto Big Field. Most of the onlookers were on the far side of the ground, boys standing or sprawling on the grass, masters and their wives in canvas deck-chairs. Near to him, however, a small spotty boy was leaning against a wall, hands in pockets. At Bognor's approach, he took his hands out of his pockets and stood to attention. Then, seeing that Bognor was not a member of staff, he put his hands back in his pockets and slumped back against the wall.

"Is this Potters?" asked Bognor, feeling fatuous.

The small boy gave him a look of withering contempt. Bognor withered and tried again. "What's the score?"

"Bassingthwaite need another ten."

Bognor looked at the score-board and saw that Bassingthwaite were a hundred and sixty-two for the loss of nine wickets.

"And the last pair in?"

"But one of them's Hodgkiss Ma," said the boy.

"Good, is he, Hodgkiss?"

"Made a hundred against Fraffleigh," said the boy.

Even as they spoke, one of the batsmen leant into his stroke and played what the professional commentators always call a "cultured" cover drive for four. Amid the ripple of clapping that greeted this shot, Bognor heard a familiar voice call out.

"Oh, well played, Hodgkiss!" Following the direction of the shout Bognor saw Peter Crutwell. Bassingthwaite's housebeak was sprawled in a deck-chair whose stripes were no more alarmingly vivid than those of the blazer that covered his upper half. On his head he wore a creamy panama hat with, though Bognor found this surprising since the society's sporting affiliations and interests were non-existent, an Arkwright and Blennerhasset ribbon tied round it. Beside him, also in white flannels but hatless and with a more subdued blazer, was Ian Edgware. Both men had pipes clutched in their fists. They looked indeed as if they might have been advertising pipe tobacco, so resolutely masculine, conservative, traditional and British did they appear. Bognor remembered Rook's remarks about "Bertie Wooftahs" and found them hard to credit now that he was on Big Field watching Potters. Murder, homosexuality, Russian agents and all the unsavoury shenanigans of the last few days seemed to belong to another, bloodier, world. Yet, if Rook was to be believed, these were the very men who had turned the Apocrypha Choir School into a prostitution racket.

"Oh, well," sighed Bognor, "only one way to find out." And he began to walk slowly round the boundary rope in the direction of the spectators. As he walked, play, of course, progressed.

The Bassingthwaite boys were moving as circumspectly as Bognor himself. Occasionally Bognor stopped to watch as the runs accumulated in a trickle, each one greeted with handclaps and a shout from Crutwell. Bognor hoped his interest in Hodgkiss Ma did not go beyond the bounds of cricket.

Bognor and Bassingthwaite kept in remarkably good step, so that just as he arrived within a few yards of Crutwell's deck-chair, Hodgkiss Ma's bat described a slicing arc and the ball came off it square, in the rough direction of gully. It was not quite what he had intended, but it would do. Immediately Crutwell was on his feet, his pipe stuffed in his blazer pocket and his hands beating each other in heavy rhythmical strokes as he led a very English housemaster's chorus. "Well played, you two. *Jolly* well played. Good show, Hodgkiss. You too, Lorimer. Well played, all of you. Jolly well done, Bassingthwaite. Thoroughly good team effort. Jolly fine all-round show." All this interspersed with the rhythmic clap of the hands, a sort of marking time. Edgware standing at his friend's shoulder was rather more subdued. He merely clapped, pipe rammed between his teeth and smoking slightly, an expression of quiet approval on his manly features. Bognor, so caught up in the occasion that he found himself clapping too, walked slowly up to them and insinuated himself in the middle.

"Good show," said Bognor. "Smashing finish."

"Jolly good show," echoed Edgware, somehow getting the words coherently through clenched lips and round his pipe.

"*Bloody* fine show," said Crutwell. "First time Bassingthwaite's won Potters since Fothergill's time."

And then, still clapping, Crutwell and Edgware turned to look at the man in the middle, this third spectator who had just joined them. Bognor grinned at them both in turn, pleased at their sudden discomfiture.

"I really enjoyed that," said Bognor, still clapping. "Unexpected bonus. Who'd have thought I'd have caught the dying moment of Potters on my first-ever visit to Ampleside?"

"Oh," said Crutwell, "it's you."

"Hello," said Edgware, removing the pipe from his teeth and smiling nervously. "What brings you to Ampleside?"

"Ah!" said Bognor. "Well, that's a long and complicated story. I'm going to have to tell it, though. Do you have a moment?"

"Well"—Crutwell frowned—"the chaps are going off for high tea now, and then there's prep. I suppose I can give you until prayers."

"Which are when?"

"Nine."

"That should be fine," said Bognor, thinking that he could, in that case, take in a swift pint at one of the attractive Ampleside pubs before getting a late train home. It seemed an age since he had seen Monica, he reflected. In fact, it would be distinctly agreeable to be able to put his feet up and enjoy a few hours of undisturbed peace and quiet.

"You're free, Ian?" Crutwell asked Edgware, and Edgware nodded. "If you'll excuse me a sec while I have a quick word with my chaps, I'll be with you in half a mo," he continued, and walked off jauntily to give his victorious team a fatherly personal man-to-man shake of the hand, pat on the back, and general all-round housemaster's approbation.

"Funny seeing Peter in his natural habitat," said Edgware quietly. "He lives for his boys."

"Yes," agreed Bognor, watching this latter-day Mr. Chips doing his stuff. "He's obviously very good at it."

"Oh, yes," said Edgware. "He'll go right to the top. The very top. Barring accidents."

"Barring accidents," repeated Bognor.

"I do hope," said Edgware, fixing Bognor with an unblinking and most meaningful stare, "that there aren't going to be any accidents."

"I hope not too," said Bognor.

"I always think Apocrypha is a wonderful sort of freemasonry. Wherever you go, wherever you are, there's always an Apocrypha man to help you out."

"Not in the Board of Trade, I'm afraid," said Bognor. "I'm the only Apocrypha man there. Certainly the only one in Special Investigations."

"No. I suppose not." Edgware smiled weakly.

"But I do see," countered Bognor, "that in a place like the Foreign Office the Apocrypha Mafia may count for rather more.

"I wouldn't call it a Mafia," said Edgware.

"Oh," said Bognor coldly, "wouldn't you?"

Before this exchange could become any more frigid, they were rejoined by Peter Crutwell, who was rubbing his hands together and oozing euphoria from every pore.

"Tell you what," he said, "why don't we take a shufti across Sneath's Meadow and see if there's a crowd at the Duck and Drake. I think this calls for a pint of shandy."

Bognor was not going to drink shandy, but provided he could have bitter he was perfectly happy to fall in with this. A crowd, on the other hand, could be embarrassing. This was not the sort of conversation which anyone would want overheard.

"Well," said Crutwell as they began to pace slowly towards the pub, "what exactly does bring you here? I can't believe it's simply the magic appeal of Potters."

"No," said Bognor. "I've come about the murder."

"I see." Crutwell put on a solemn, almost melancholy face, which Bognor guessed he used for lecturing boys prior to beating them. If beating boys was allowed, still.

"What about the murder, exactly?"

"You must realise that everyone who was drinking with the Master that night is a suspect?"

"Including you?"

"Including me."

They were approaching a river lined with willows, recently pollarded. Cows grazed on the further bank. A wooden foot-bridge spanned the stream which flowed fast enough to create little swirling patterns on the surface, eddies among the reeds. A couple, entwined, were strolling towards them. It was very quiet, very pastoral, very English.

"You sure he was murdered?" asked Edgware. "Seems awfully melodramatic."

"Quite sure," said Bognor. "As for melodrama, yes, I'm afraid things have been rather melodramatic lately. Sebastian Vole's been killed and Max Aveline almost certainly did it. He's fled to Russia. He's a sort of supercharged Philby, it seems. But you'll read all about that in tomorrow's papers. Even I was attacked."

"I thought you looked a bit seedy," said Edgware sympathetically. "What happened?"

"Someone ambushed me at the Randolph."

"Ah!"

They crossed the bridge. No one spoke. Bognor noticed a pair of ducks diving for food, bottoms waggling absurdly in the air every time they submerged themselves. Crutwell turned left, hands deep in pockets, head slumped forward, evidently deep in thought.

"Where've you been, by the way?" asked Bognor. "I could have sworn I saw you in the High the other day. Either of you have a scarlet Range Rover?"

"Yes," said Crutwell. "I take it on digs. Actually, it nominally belongs to the school archaeological society but it's licenced in my name."

"Was it you?"

"No," said Crutwell.

"Yes," said Edgware.

Another longer silence ensued, more pregnant this time. Ahead of them Bognor could see a thatched whitewashed building with an Inn sign outside, as well as a scattering of picnic tables, all but one unoccupied.

Crutwell relit his pipe, an elaborate process which had the intended effect of making speech impossible. Crutwell obviously did not know what to say next and lighting his pipe was an attempt to disguise the fact. It fooled no one, not even him. Bognor, on the other hand, had no intention of making life easier for either of them by asking a direct question. Not yet.

"Quite empty," said Edgware.

They continued in silence.

Eventually, on reaching the garden, Bognor asked the others what they were drinking. Crutwell stayed with his shandy. Edgware, on the other hand, asked if Bognor would mind awfully if he were to have a gin and tonic. It was, he supposed, silly of him to give them the chance to get their act together while he fetched the drinks, but he had a hunch which told him that despite some evidence to the contrary it would be Edgware who would prevail. Edgware wanted to tell the truth, Crutwell to conceal it. Bognor felt confident that by the time he settled himself down in the garden the others would have decided that small lies would lead to greater ones and ultimately to disaster. Crutwell, used to getting away with deceptions in a world in which his word was accepted without question, was less of a realist than Edgware, whose life was founded largely on determining the extent of deception permissible in oneself and the degree of deception being attempted by others.

Returning to their table with the drinks balanced on a battered old tin tray, Bognor found that, as he had expected, an earnest confabulation had taken the place of the earlier silences, though quiet descended again at his approach.

"Cheers," he said, sitting down. The pub was a free house and sold Draught Youngs, his favourite beer. Life was looking up.

"Cheers." The two other Apocrypha men were not going to forego social niceties at a time like this.

"Look," said Edgware, carefully removing the slice of lemon from his glass and depositing it on the tray, "I'm afraid there are one or two things we have to tell you."

"Yes," said Bognor. He smiled, and wiped froth from his upper lip.

"The fact is," said Edgware, "that it *was* us you saw in the High that afternoon."

"Yes," said Bognor again, still smiling.

"We had rather hoped," went on Edgware, "that we wouldn't bump into anyone we knew."

"I see," said Bognor.

"The reason being," said Crutwell, "that we were contemplating something which wouldn't have looked very good had we been found out."

"Theft," said Bognor.

"Well"—Crutwell was looking very much as if he would have preferred something stronger than shandy—"I wouldn't put it quite like that."

"How would you put it, then?"

"Simon's quite right," said Edgware. "No point in pretending otherwise. We'd come up to Oxford to steal something."

"Files from the Master's office."

"Yes."

"But when you got there," said Bognor helpfully, "you found that someone had been there before you."

"Yes."

"Would you mind," asked Bognor gently, for vestiges of affection and respect for his college, its good name, its former members and general *esprit de corps* still remained in him, "would you mind telling me why you were so keen to get those files that you were actually prepared to nick them?"

"I imagine you know that by now," said Crutwell aggressively.

"I want you to tell me," said Bognor.

"Either he knows or he doesn't know," said Crutwell to Edgware. "I'm damned if I see why we should make his job any easier, let alone incriminate ourselves unnecessarily."

Edgware paid no immediate attention. "Presumably you've read the files?"

"What makes you say that?"

"Well"—Edgware shrugged—"it's ridiculous to suggest otherwise."

"Suppose I were to tell you I hadn't got the files?"

"We wouldn't believe you."

"I haven't got the files."

"I *don't* believe you," said Edgware angrily. "Stop playing around, please. You're not making this easy."

"I don't want to make it easy," snapped Bognor. "You didn't think about that when you hit me at the Randolph. You could have bloody killed me."

"It was Peter," said Edgware. "He panicked."

"I'm having a Scotch," said Crutwell suddenly. "Anybody else?"

Edgware asked for another gin, Bognor another pint.

"Leaving aside the whereabouts of the files," said Bognor, as Crutwell disappeared towards the bar, "you went to my room because you assumed I'd got them."

"Yes," said Edgware. "We had a long talk about it. In the end, it did at least seem worth a try. But I assume the police had them."

"No. As it happens, Vole had them."

"Vole?"

"Presumably he took them to further his researches. We'll never know. He made an awful mess of the Master's study. I should have thought that would warn you that it wasn't me. We would have been slightly more professional. You too, come to that. Don't they teach breaking and entering at the FO?"

Edgware smiled stiffly. "Yes, but not in the public schools. Peter's admirable in most respects, but he'll never make a burglar."

"Hmmm. Nor a headmaster now."

"What do you mean?"

Bognor raised his eyebrows. As he did, Crutwell emerged

from the door of the pub carrying his round of drinks. He looked, in his gaudy cricket outfit, like the twelfth man carrying refreshment out to the players. Perhaps, thought Bognor, that's exactly what he's doing. Perhaps life is just a game of cricket. In which case, both Edgware and Crutwell had thrown away their wickets at a crucial stage in their innings. Just when they looked set for a century apiece. Silly. Careless.

Bognor took a large mouthful, suppressed a belch and decided to come briskly to the point.

"The files are in Moscow," he said, "with Aveline. Which means that your guilty secret can hardly be said to be safe. Now it's perfectly plain that both of you are in grave trouble, but I'm not sure that you realise how grave. It's not just a matter of your careers, your marriages, your reputations and all that. It's a matter of murder." He paused to see if he was having the effect for which he had hoped. On balance, to judge from their chastened expressions, he was.

"Would it make it easier for you if I said that although I have not yet, and I emphasise *yet*, had a chance to examine the files myself, I have been given an account of the business of you two and the College Choir School? I don't want to indulge in any gratuitous muck-raking. I just need to confirm that, broadly speaking, it's true."

He looked from one to the other. Neither spoke. Both nodded.

"O.K.," he said. "Ian was awaiting preferment at the FO, and Peter was hoping to get the headmastership of Fraffleigh. And you thought Beckenham would ruin your chances. Correct?"

"No," said Edgware with vehemence. "It's very much not it. The point is that as long as Beckenham was around we knew he wouldn't shop us. It was a long time ago, it was deeply shocking and all that but it's over, it's in the past. Beckenham accepted that. If he'd died naturally with some sort of warning he would presumably have destroyed any records that incriminated us. I would think he'd destroy the files when he finished being Master. But that's just speculation. Peter and I had a shrewd idea that the files contained trouble as far as we were concerned and we were desperately worried in case they fell into the wrong hands."

"I see." Bognor was suddenly depressed. Another failure loomed.

"You admit," he said, "that you came back to Oxford, broke into the Master's lodgings and then into my room at the Randolph, where you attacked me."

"I really am sorry about that, old man," said Crutwell. "Lost me nerve."

Bognor grimaced ruefully. "But you deny having killed the Master?"

"I grant you," said Edgware, "that from a circumstantial point of view we may have to be included on your list of suspects. But as I've tried to point out, we have no motive. Lord Beckenham always played straight with us. He'd given us references before and they'd always been glowing. There was no reason to think that they wouldn't go on being glowing."

"Even," said Bognor, "when the jobs were as significant as the ones you're up for? I mean, he may have been prepared to countenance the idea of having you in positions of middling power and influence, but to connive at someone with that sort of skeleton in their past getting the headmastership of Fraffleigh . . . Well, surely he'd have drawn the line somewhere? I mean . . ." He gulped beer. Words failed him. The sun was going down. In more ways than one.

"I think," said Crutwell, seeming to regain a modicum of self-confidence, "that the Master had more, how shall I put it, vision, yes I think that's the word, more *vision* than you credit him with. If he believed, as I think he did, that I was suitable to be headmaster of one of our great English public schools, then I don't think he'd dredge up some peccadillo from the past in order to prevent it. And the same applies to Ian. The Master clearly thought Ian should go to the very, very top and that the country would frankly be damned lucky to be represented by a man of Ian's outstanding intellect and character. Why should he suddenly throw all that into jeopardy? It simply doesn't make sense. Beckenham was a great man in his way and, like a lot of great men, he saw beyond detail. The little things of life didn't mean anything. He was interested in big things, Simon. He had *big* ideas, *big* hopes. He wanted to transform the world and we were to be his instruments. He was like Milner. He nurtured his protégés because he believed in them. He believed in us. He believed in our contribution to the future. We made a mistake. A bad mistake. But he forgave us and he set it aside, because he was a *big* man."

Bognor decided he was going mad. There was no alternative.

"Forgive me," he said incredulously, "but did you say 'peccadillo.'"

"We were very young, Simon." Edgware, at least, had the diplomat's concern to appear reasonable at all times. "Of course, what we did was reprehensible, but what Peter is really saying is that the Master made his own judgements about people and once he'd made them he stuck with them. He was very consistent and very loyal, and we repaid that loyalty and that consistency."

Bognor could take no more. "I used to think," he said, voice trembling but, still, just controlled, "that I quite liked old Beckenham. I knew he didn't rate me very highly, but he didn't seem to actively dislike me and he was always polite. I knew he thought Rook and you two were the great white hopes of our generation, and because I was absurdly naïve I suppose I went along with that. Now it turns out that Rook was a liar and a cheat and that you two were venal pederasts of the most revolting sort imaginable. And that he knew all along. You were all as bad as each other." He got to his feet. "All right," he said, "so you didn't kill him. Frankly, I begin to wish you had. But just because I can't pin that on you, don't think you're going to get away with this. I'm not totally without influence and I promise you that I shall do everything—everything—in my power to ensure that the pair of you languish in the obscurity you so richly deserve."

And still quivering with rage and lost illusion he lunged off into the twilight. Behind him he left the housemaster and the diplomat contemplating each other in amazement that such innocence and altruism could still stalk the land, even though it was confined to the lower regions of the Board of Trade.

CHAPTER 8

It was a relief to be home with Monica. Gadding about was all very well for a time and in its way, but Bognor was essentially a lethargic animal dedicated to creature comforts. His most besetting sin was sloth, and what he really liked was warmth, security, predictability and a quiet life. There were moments when he wished he were a gayer (in the true sense) blade, but he knew that he was not cut out for it. True, he lusted in a wistful way after leggy ladies like Dr. Frinton, but when it came to the point, he tended to find them more alarming than alluring, and he would be disconcerted to wake up with a strange face beside him every morning. Monica was putting on weight. The line of her jaw was not as firm as once it was, but then no one could accuse *him* of being an oil painting. He had never been more than a water-colour even in his prime, and he was now firmly in the lithograph class, in an unlimited edition, too. Still, for all his faults, he was basically nice, in the same sort of way that Rook, Crutwell and Edgware were deep-down nasty. Monica was nice too. Both had a considerable capacity for naughtiness but not, he liked to think, for evil. They were capable of infinite sorts of over-indulgence but never of malice. They were well suited to each other, fitted each other like old gloves, though it did them good to get away from each other occasionally, if only because the reunions were so agreeable.

It was with thoughts such as these racketing around his mind that he let himself into the flat after the upsetting trip to Ampleside. Monica was in bed reading *Phineas Redux*.

"Hello, you," she said. "Have you eaten?"

"Had a pork pie on the train," he said. He had eaten two Mars Bars, too, but thought it better not to admit to them.

They kissed. "Missed you," he said.

"Me too."

They kissed again.

"You don't look too hot," she said, pushing him away to get a sense of perspective on him.

"Not too hot," he said, "as a matter of fact. Tell you what, why don't I make us both a mug of chocolate and I'll tell you all about it?"

"With marshmallow."

"All right."

In the end it was she, taking pity on his fragile and battered appearance, who made the chocolate, while he changed into his striped pyjamas. Then they both clambered into bed and sat up drinking chocolate while Bognor told his story.

"Aveline," said Monica when he got to the Regius Professor. "Did you say Aveline?"

"Yes."

"Professor Max Aveline?"

"Yes. Why?"

"Because he just called. It was a terrible line. Sounded as if he was in Siberia."

"He probably was. Are you sure it was Aveline?"

"Almost. It was a really rotten line, but I'm virtually certain he said his name was Professor Max Aveline."

Bognor stared at the frothy marshmallow on top of his drink.

"I think I may be about to become lucky," he said, kissing the tip of his wife's nose. "What did he say?"

"Wanted to know when you'd be home and said he'd ring back later. Sounded rather over-excited."

"I dare say he did," said Bognor. "It's catching, too. I think I'm about to become over-excited myself."

"Explain," said Monica. "You haven't finished."

Fifteen minutes later, having included everything except one or two details concerning Molly Mortimer and Hermione Frinton, he said, "So that's it."

"Quite a story," she said, snuggling up to him. "Let me look," and she peered into his hair like a mother monkey inspecting for fleas.

"Ouch!" she exclaimed. "Nasty."

"Thanks," he said. "Some people have been inclined to laugh at my wounds and make out that three stitches are a trivial matter."

"Not me. Looks horrid."

"For once I agree with Rook. They are a pair of extremely disagreeable Bertie Wooftahs, and I intend sorting them out."

"You do just that." She giggled.

"What time did Aveline say he'd phone again?"

"He didn't. I just told him you'd be in before midnight."

Bognor glanced at his watch and even as he did the phone shrilled. He picked it up at once. "Bognor," he snapped in his most official manner. Static, crackling, clicks and alien tongues assaulted his ears. Bognor put his hand over the mouthpiece. "I think he's lost his rubles," he said. He removed his hand and addressed himself to the phone. "Hello!" he called. "Hello! Hello! Hello! Moscow, can you hear me?"

Down the line a woman's voice answered him back. "London! London! Hello, London, can you hear me? This is Moscow calling." The voice faded and was replaced by more breakfast-cereal noises, then just as Bognor was about to put the machine down in despair the line became miraculously cleared and the donnishly English Regius Professor of Sociology was saying, "Bognor . . . Bognor . . . is that you? God, the bloody phones in this bloody country are worse than the bloody phones in bloody England."

"Yes," said Bognor. "Hello, yes, it's me. Bognor here. Bognor speaking."

"Can you hear me? It's three o'clock in the bloody morning here."

"It's midnight here."

"I didn't phone to discuss the time. What's this about my having murdered Beckenham?"

"What?"

"It's a very bad line." Aveline was shouting. "I can't hear you. What?"

"I don't know anything about your having murdered Beckenham," said Bognor. "I assume you had poor Sebastian Vole done away with, but I know nothing about your having killed Beckenham. Did you?"

"That's what I'm ringing to tell you. It's unfortunate about Vole. We had no alternative. He'd been very conscientious and surprisingly astute, but that's by the way. I wish to make it absolutely plain that I did not kill Beckenham. Beckenham was a valued colleague. To say that I killed him is the grossest calumny."

Bognor didn't think it possible to calumnize a former Regius who turned out to be a traitor and a murderer.

"How do you know all this anyway?" asked Bognor.

"I'm told by my friends that the *Daily Globe* are publishing a story tomorrow. I assumed it was a leak inspired by you and your friend Dr. Frinton."

"Far from it."

There was a snort of disbelief from the Moscow end. "I do not propose to be a scapegoat for your incompetence."

"All right"—Bognor bridled—"if you didn't do it, then who the hell did?"

"I wouldn't expect you to believe me," said Aveline. "However, a colleague of mine will be in touch with you as soon as possible. I spoke to him earlier this evening. It was he who tipped me off. He'll tell you who Beckenham's murderer was. I can't identify him beyond saying that he will call himself 'Q.' He is a senior officer of British Intelligence, but you won't know him. I think you'll believe him, though. You'll find he knows more about you than you yourself. That's all. He'll be in touch. Good night."

Bognor stared at the receiver with disbelief. "Would you believe it?" he asked eventually. "That bastard Aveline is trying to clear his name."

"How do you mean?" asked Monica. "If he's in Moscow he can hardly deny being one of theirs."

"No, not that," said Bognor. "He's not the least bit ashamed of that. Nor of having old Vole killed. But he doesn't want it to be thought he killed the Master."

"And did he?"

"God knows." He finished the dregs of his now rather cold cocoa, and put the mug on the bedside table. "Someone called 'Q' is going to be in touch."

"Q?" Monica giggled. "Who he?"

"Something in intelligence. Our intelligence. Theirs too, I presume. A triple agent at least."

He turned out the light. "If you want my opinion," he said, "there's no intelligent life in intelligence."

"Ha bloody ha," she scoffed.

He silenced her with a kiss.

"Ugh," she said struggling free, "you reek of chocolate."

Next morning there was a note on the doormat along with a gas bill, a final demand from Barclaycard and a circular from a mail order firm offering life-size reproductions of sculpture by Moore, Hepworth and Elizabeth Frink made from reinforced papier mâché. The note, typed on a manual portable, said: "Round Pond. 11. Will be wearing A and B tie. Q."

"Can't get more cryptic than that," said Bognor, showing it to Monica, who read it three times, held it up to the light and finally said, "Oh, do be careful, Simon."

"Careful? How do you mean, careful?"

"I mean, don't get shot or abducted."

"In Kensington Gardens? Be your age."

"I *am*. The Iranian Embassy's only just down the road. If this man really is a triple agent there's no telling what he may get up to. There are corpses all over the place in this case, Simon, so for heaven's sake be careful."

"If anything awful happens I'll scream blue murder and hordes of hirsute Norland nannies will attack the hapless Q with raised umbrellas. Led by Wendy Craig, no doubt."

"Now you're being ridiculous."

"Not in the least. I feel in the mood for toast. If I'm going to be shot by this anonymous figure in Arkwright and Blennerhasset neckwear, I might as well eat a hearty breakfast."

"I do wish you wouldn't be frivolous." Monica sighed and went to percolate coffee and titivate.

An hour or so later, Bognor sauntered up Kensington High Street past the Royal Garden Hotel and through the gates of the Gardens. It was hot. One or two au pairs, not at all nubile, sunned themselves on the grass in bikinis. Men in abbreviated bathing trunks with oily olive skins and muscles disported themselves similarly. Waiters, thought Bognor, pulling his stomach in and trying to appear jaunty. He smiled cheekily at a big-busted blonde in an emerald green job which reminded him of Hermione Frinton's All Souls' leotard and was upset when she turned away contemptuously. He really must be getting old.

At the pond there was the usual gaggle of exceedingly rich infants in superannuated perambulators attended by nursemaids and nannies in starched uniforms. Older children and pensioners played with boats, many of them remote-controlled. And on one of the benches, reading a copy of *Now!* magazine, sat a small grey man in a pink and purple tie.

"So that's 'Q,'" thought Bognor. He was very small, rather neat, quite unrecognisable. The sort of man who merged. He would never be noticeable. Never be out of place. As Bognor contemplated him from afar, he looked up and smiled. It was an oddly attractive smile. Bognor had not anticipated meeting a likeable man and yet he felt an unexpected warmth from this man. He could have been any age over sixty, white-haired, heavily lined, but amused in appearance and, Bognor thought, probably amusing, too.

He folded the magazine and placed it alongside him on the park bench, then looked up again and smiled. Bognor noticed for the first time that he had a little silvery goatee beard. He did not move. Bognor was obviously supposed to go to him. He did.

"Morning, Simon," said the man, very nonchalantly, as if this meeting was a pleasant, unremarkable coincidence and Bognor an old friend. "Pray sit."

Bognor sat.

"I was sorry," said "Q," "to hear about your mother's cat."

Bognor winced. His mother's cat had been run over a fortnight before. In Letchworth. Hardly anyone knew he had a mother. Not even Parkinson. And scarcely one of those who knew he had a mother knew the mother had a cat.

"It was a quite old cat," said Bognor, "smelly, too. Can't say I cared for it."

"Your application for transfer by the way . . ." The little man shook his head. "You're far too valuable where you are, you know. I fear you're there for life. Whatever Parkinson may think."

"Look," said Bognor, "who *are* you? And who . . . and why . . . and are you entitled to wear that tie?" It was an odd question to ask, but there was something *un*-Apocryphal about him which was disturbing. "Just call me 'Q,'" he said. "Better that way. And since you ask, I suppose I'm not, strictly speaking, entitled to the tie. No. Does it matter?"

Bognor said he supposed not. The man laughed at this. He had a cane which he picked up and used to beat the tarmac with. It was wooden, ash perhaps, with a silver handle. Could have been a sword-stick. "Q" could have been a fencer. He had an agile air.

"Well," said "Q," "I'll be brief. Are you ready to believe?"

"I'm not sure," said Bognor. "I don't care for this secrecy. I don't like to believe what I hear from a man with no name. Do you have any proof of identity? A card? A letter? Can't I know more? Whose side are you on? Ours or theirs?"

"Q" seemed to consider this very seriously for a minute or two, and then he said, solemnly, "I don't think I can answer that. You see, at my level of intelligence work the question ceases to have meaning. I work to please myself. I have no other master. Contacts, friends, allegiances, alliances . . . But sides? I prefer not to take sides."

"I see." Bognor was perplexed. At the same time he knew a cul-de-sac when he saw one. "O.K.," he said. "You have a message for me. I'm disposed to believe it. I have precious little alternative. Go ahead. Tell me."

"You realise Aveline's defection is a national scandal?"

Bognor had read the *Globe*, seen the breakfast news and heard Peter Jay's homily. "I suppose," he said.

"I have no particular brief for Aveline," said "Q," "though he'll be much maligned, and he has an honesty of sorts. For myself, I like to see records as straight as possible, so I tell you this and leave you to decide what to do with the information. First, I do not believe that Aveline killed Lord Beckenham."

"No?" Bognor watched a five-year-old in a sailor suit whirl an electric trimaran through a figure of eight.

"No," said "Q," and paused. "You're too young to remember the Mitovan affair?"

"If you say so."

"I say so," said "Q." "Mitovan was a Yugoslav. Wrong to call him Serb or Croat or anything else. He was before his time. Killed. Betrayed."

"When?"

"Oh, during the war. The British parachuted him in. He had come out in 1938 with his younger brother." "Q" raised his stick and beat the ground three times hard. "Bad business," he said.

"And who betrayed him?"

"You can't guess?" Quizzical blue eyes peered into his, almost laughing, yet too compassionate for cheap laughter. "We didn't know at the time, of course, and by the time we found out it was too late. In fact, it was much neater to leave him in place."

"The complexity of intelligence operations never ceases to baffle me," said Bognor sourly.

"Never ceases to baffle us all," said "Q." "Otherwise, we'd all be a sight better at it, wouldn't you say?" He laughed again, an attractive punctuation mark. "No," he said, "it's too serious to tease. Mitovan was betrayed by the man who later became Lord Beckenham."

"I see," said Bognor.

"Your old friend Vole had got hold of it, of course. He came to see me a couple of times. That book of his would have been remarkable, though I doubt now whether it will ever see the light of day." He paused and gazed ruminatively at the boats on the pond. "There are certain things, I'm afraid," and he spoke sadly now, "which are better left unsaid. Offends a few principles one may hold, but can't be helped."

Bognor prompted him gently. "I had got the picture about Beckenham," he said, "but I don't think I fully understand where this business about the Yugoslav gets us."

"Mitovan," said "Q," "was an attractive man, very. He'd have given Tito something to think about but, well, the Germans put him in one of the camps. Doesn't bear thinking about, really. I don't believe he ever talked, despite what they did to him . . ."

Bognor allowed the silence to drift for a moment and then said again, plaintively, "Yes, but . . ."

"Mitovan," repeated "Q." "Doesn't that mean anything? Ring no bells?"

"No," said Bognor, "I don't know any Yugoslavs."

"You do, in a manner of speaking. Remember, I said he had a young brother he brought out of the Balkans with him. All the rest of the family had been massacred."

"Yes, but I still don't see . . ."

"Perhaps," said "Q," "my pronunciation is misleading. Jo was always keen to stress that last syllable, but when his brother changed the name he put all the emphasis up the front."

"Mitovan," said Bognor. "You don't mean . . . ?"

"That's exactly who I mean," said "Q." "I know what you're thinking, but it often affects people like that. He is a little more English than the English, but that's not uncommon. It takes foreigners like Daninoa and Mikes to really caricature the English. We're not nearly so extreme."

"And you think he avenged his brother."

"In fact, I know," said "Q" very seriously now. "But listen to me." He bent his head low and spoke very softly to the younger man. "The slate is clean. It was the only honourable course. It's right that you should know. How right it is for others to know, I'm not certain. That's for you to decide. It's your case. Yours and Dr. Frinton's. I'm sure you'll make the right decision."

He stood. "Good-bye, then," he said. "I don't suppose we shall meet again. And, by the way, don't be too hard on poor Parkinson. He does his best." And with a trace of a smile, more evident in the eyes than around the mouth, "Q" waved his cane, turned and vanished among the nannies and their charges.

Bognor sat on the bench for a moment, then ran to the park gates and hailed a taxi for Paddington Station.

He reached Apocrypha Great Gate shortly after two and hurried at once to Mitten's rooms. They were empty. He then walked briskly across the quad to Dr. Frinton's rooms. There was no one there, either. He had not banked on this. The revelations of "Q" were too sensitive and explosive to be entrusted to the public telephone. He had had to make personal contact. Now the only two people to whom he needed to talk had disappeared. There was the Chief Inspector Chappie, but against much of his training and many of his inclinations he had decided that the Inspector's involvement was going to have to be prematurely curtailed. This was one time when town was going to be rigorously excluded by gown. It smacked of privilege, of the age-old arrogance of Apocrypha, and Bognor was deeply unhappy about it. On this sad occasion, however, he could think of no alternative.

He walked back to the Lodge and asked the porter if Mr. Mitten was in college.

"Yes, sir."

"But he's not in his rooms?"

"No, sir. He's in the Senior Common Room."

"And Dr. Frinton?"

"Yes, sir."

"What? She's in the SCR too? In that case, I'll pop along and dig them out."

"I wouldn't do that, sir."

"Oh. Why not?" The porter seemed surprisingly serious. Bognor frowned. He hoped there hadn't been any more corpses since he left town.

"It's a college meeting."

"That's all right. They're probably only talking about drains. They'll be glad to be hauled out."

"Not drains they're talking about this time, sir." He bent down to the small hole in the glass between them. "It's the Mastership," he said *sotto voce*. "I believe they're electing Lord Beckenham's successor."

Bognor swore. This was indecent haste. Beckenham hardly cold and already they were electing someone to take his place. On the other hand, the rumour and speculation and scandal were so rife that speed might seem to some Fellows to be essential. He tried to think straight. If they were carrying out an election this early, there would have been no time to wheel out the host of impressive outside candidates from Whitehall, Westminster and the BBC who usually jostled for jobs like this. They could only be meeting to elect an internal candidate, and the most obvious internal candidate by far was Mitten himself. In fact, you might say it was the merest of formalities. "Oh, bloody hell," he said and swung round and ran off towards the common room.

The Apocrypha Common Room was actually a complex of rooms, the first of which was a straightforward entrance hall. The door was locked and it was opened after repeated knocking by the formidable figure of Bell, the College Butler. Bell allowed him into the hall but no further.

"This is vital," snapped Bognor, who had never liked Bell even when he was a relatively junior Scout during his own undergraduate days. "It is a matter of life and death, not to mention the good name of the college."

The good name of the college meant much more to Bell than life and death but he was not to be swayed. He remembered Bognor as well as Bognor remembered him, and with no more enthusiasm. It was clear to both men that this was what contemporary jargon would call an "irresistible force—immovable object" situation. Bognor realised that he had no more chance of getting into the election meeting than he would have had of making it into the Sistine Chapel when the Cardinals were choosing a pope. "If," he suggested, "I give you a note for Dr. Frinton, will you deliver it?"

Bell seemed to consider this for an age, but eventually he said he supposed there was no harm in it. Hastily Bognor ripped a page from his diary and scribbled the message: "Mitten dunnit. Total gen. Am outside. Come quick. Bognor Board of Trade."

He supposed Bell would read it, but that was too bad. With any luck, he wouldn't understand it. The next few minutes passed excruciatingly slowly. Bognor paced and tried to collect his thoughts, but they were hopelessly and irretrievably confused. At last the note worked. Bell came out with Hermione in tow. She was wearing *haute couture* jeans, her MA gown and an expression of extreme irritation. Bognor thought she had never looked lovelier.

"Darling," she said, waving his note at him, "what is all this rot? It had better be good. We're just about to vote."

Bognor closed his eyes. "You must not vote. You must absolutely not vote. It would be a disaster for the college."

"I can't agree," she said. "Best to get it out of the way. Waldy will make a perfectly adequate Master and we can't stand any more two-ring circuses at the moment."

"But you can't elect a man who has just murdered his predecessor," hissed Bognor. "It'll be like the Wars of the Roses."

"I think you had better explain," said Dr. Frinton in a voice that would have doused the fires of hell.

Bognor did, rapidly, skidding round corners, taking the facts at reckless speed but wrapping the whole story up in not much more than five minutes flat.

"You mean Waldegrave is a Yugoslav?" she said. "But that's preposterous. He's no more Yugoslav than you or I. If he's a Yugoslav, then I'm a virgin."

"It's true."

"You're off your rocker, darling."

"You can be a very obstinate and silly woman," he said. "There is more to life than *Beowulf* and Bolislav." He tore another page from his diary. "If you won't believe me, maybe *he* will." And he scribbled another note. "I know everything," it said. "Please come out now. Bognor." He folded it up and wrote on the outside, "Mr. Mitovan."

The next few minutes of pacing seemed even longer than the last, but at length the door to the electoral chamber was opened and Waldegrave Mitten came out on his own. He was looking, appropriately yet paradoxically, extraordinarily English in his shabby tweed jacket and a canary-coloured cardigan. Bognor saw at once that his hands, at least metaphorically speaking, were up.

"I'm sorry," said Bognor.

"I can't say I am," said Mitten. "It was too good for him, going like that."

"You can't be Master, I'm afraid."

"To be honest, it's rather a relief."

Mitten smiled and Bognor smiled back, one Apocrypha man to another.

"So you see," said Bognor, squeezing lemon onto his smoked salmon, "I've connived in a cover-up."

His wife frowned. She had a stuffed leg of lamb *en croûte* in the oven, to go with the celebratory Château Cantemerle.

"Isn't it a bit of a risk," she said, "and, well, without being puritanical about it, well, *wrong?*"

"He only killed him," said Bognor.

"That's what I mean."

"Aveline and Beckenham killed lots of people. Or had them killed."

"And the poor Chief Inspector Chappie doesn't suspect anything?"

"I think he does suspect a little"—Bognor's eyes glazed as he contemplated the exquisite fish—"but he knows he's outranked. National Security is more important than common or garden justice."

"I don't like the sound of that," said Monica.

"No," said Bognor, "but there's justice and justice. I think it's been done, and if Aveline is credited with one extra piece of bloodiness, who cares except him? Besides, it's useful propaganda if the world believes that Soviet moles are given to knocking each other off when the going gets rough."

"I suppose so," said Monica. She seemed dubious.

"And I have also had a word with the right people about

Edgware, Crutwell and Rook," said Bognor with satis-faction. "There's a spanner in their works all right."

"And Mitten keeps his job at Apocrypha?"

"Absolutely. They'll just have to find a new Master from somewhere else." Bognor chewed thoughtfully. "They need a sound, reliable, decent Old Apocrypha man of integrity, ability . . ." He drank a little Gewürtz-traminer and rolled it round his mouth. "Do you suppose," he asked, "that Parkinson would give me a decent reference?"

This is Tim Heald's seventh novel to feature Simon Bognor, and his second for the Crime Club. His previous novels include *Let Sleeping Dogs Die, Deadline, Unbecoming Habits, Blue Blood Will Out,* and *Just Desserts.* He is also the author of the novel *Caroline R,* and, with Mayo Mohs, a biography of Prince Charles called *HRH: The Man Who Will Be King.* As a journalist, he has written numerous profiles of such subjects as the British Royal Family, Pierre and Margaret Trudeau, and Richard Burton. Mr. Heald (and Simon Bognor) made his Crime Club debut with *Murder at Moose Jaw* in October 1981.